CLACKAMAS LITERARY REVIEW

2011
Volume XV

Clackamas Community College
Oregon City, Oregon

CLACKAMAS LITERARY REVIEW

Editor in Chief
Ryan Davis

Associate Editor
Heather Frazier

Assistant Editor
Amy Filener

Cover Art
Lorna Nakell
"Flying Night"

Journal Design
Matthew Warren

The Clackamas Literary Review is published annually at Clackamas Community College. Manuscripts are read from September 1st to January 31st and will not be returned. By submitting your work to *CLR*, you indicate your consent for us to publish that work in print and online. This issue is $10; issues I–XI are $6 if ordered through *CLR*; issues XII–XIV are available through your favorite online bookseller.

Clackamas Literary Review
19600 Molalla Avenue, Oregon City, Oregon 97045
ISBN: 978-0-9796882-3-2
Printed by Lightning Source
www.clackamasliteraryreview.org

CONTENTS

CONTRIBUTORS

Editor in Chief's Note

The 2011 volume of *Clackamas Literary Review* is full of the mysterious, the speculative, or maybe it's just full of the lies we tell ourselves. In Iris Miller's poem, her narrator admittedly stretches the truth that frames the narrative. Just a few stanzas later, the narrator tells us, "This story is true," which makes us question not only the poem but ourselves because we know how memory works. Poet Bill Jolliff tells us a "magical" story about a cowboy who went west but didn't remain because "Maybe heaven is an easier place to get to / than to stay," which is most likely true. Talia Carner, in her essay, grapples to understand the housekeeper she no longer employs, but still sends money to eighteen years later. She is on a quest to understand a part of herself, much like the protagonist in Lawrence F. Farrar's short story. This character reaches out, is taken advantage of, and wonders not only why he was suckered, but why he made himself vulnerable in the first place. Greg Evason's poem "7 Mini Fictions" begins with "Once upon a time" and ends with "A long time ago," which represents all our stories, more or less. If our truths reside in the past, which is most often murky, how can we know what really happened? This volume will help us sift out the truths we can live with.

Enjoy,
Ryan Davis
Editor in Chief

Third Way

J. Stephen Rhodes

There are three paths to happiness.
I am only going to tell you two.
But first, there once was an imam who,
every morning, dug a hole in his garden
and proceeded to stand in it,
covering his feet with soil. For an hour
he stood, arms upraised. This he did
even before kneeling toward Mecca.

> The first path to happiness
> is to go into the forest and gather sticks,
> straight and sleek. Or, if you live
> in a desert, walk and gather stones,
> preferably smooth. Stones or sticks,
> more is what you're after, but
> quality counts, too. If you live
> by the sea or on a steppe—
> I think you get the point.

Anyway, the neighbors of this imam
thought he was nuts.
Even when it rained, he stood there

every morning, arms in the air.
Because he was a holy man,
they said nothing, but in their houses
they shook their heads. They did
allow he tried to live by the laws,
and was always good to the poor.

Once you've tried the first path,
the second is simpler, at least to explain.
You know all those sticks and stones?
You give them away.

So, one day one of the neighbors
finally leaned over the garden wall
and asked, Teacher, why do you stand
every morning with your feet buried
in the ground, to which the imam said,

For years when I studied the words
of the Prophet, blessed be his name,
and tried to apply them to my life,
I was always worried about enough—
Do I have it? Do I give it?
I was constantly picking things up,
putting them back down.
Then one morning a few years ago,
while I kneeled on my sajada
in this very garden, beseeching
Allah, the Compassionate,

to show me what would suffice,
a nectarine fell from a branch
and rolled right under my nose.
I heard a voice say, Be like this tree.
So each morning, I am trying.
But as you can see, all I'm getting
are dirty feet.

The neighbor turned and walked away,
thinking to himself, what a fool—
which is why I'm not about to say
anything to you about path number three.

The Wife I Can Never Divorce

Talia Carner

There were consequences to shattering the glass ceiling with my head; cracking my own skull was one of them. Eventually, though, I healed and moved on—even changed careers—putting it all behind me. Or so I thought.

In the early 80s, dressed in a pinstripe suit, the bow at my collar mimicking my male colleagues' ties, I was clawing my way up the corporate ladder in a man's world steeped in misogyny, official gender discrimination, and corporate-endorsed sexual harassment. My first boss at *Redbook* magazine didn't even know I had children. After outshining my twenty male colleagues in annual revenues for the second year running (while earning half their salaries because "you have a husband"), I hung a photograph of my little girls on my office wall. "We don't hire mothers," my boss said upon spotting the photograph. Promoting a woman to management had never been considered before and now, with the revelation of my children's existence, I was out of the running for good. The irony that *Redbook* magazine targeted young mothers was lost on our management. Even our Editor-in-Chief was an aging man who advised millions of young women each month how to manage home, kitchen, and children. The underlying editorial assumption was that wives' sole reason to work—feminists were yet to convince the establishment that being a homemaker was "work"— was due to their husbands' failure to provide.

My daily commute from our suburban Long Island home to New York City added to the hours I was absent from home. Even as my husband Ron shouldered much of the household responsibilities, including the care of the two little girls I brought into the marriage, he had an office to run and a daughter and son of his own to shuttle about. I needed a live-in housekeeper to manage our life as a combined family. I needed a wife.

Enter Malaya. After a string of failed housekeepers, Malaya responded to my newspaper ad. A middle-aged spinster from South Africa, where her Filipino origins with the lightest tinge of African blood marked her as "colored," she had arrived in the United States ten years before with one family, and had spent the past six years with another. From the moment she entered our home, dressed in an off-white skirt suit, I liked the broad face that seemed to have been made of hard rubber. The delighted smile bunching up her cheeks as her gaze followed my preschooler who'd need most of her attention, sealed our agreement.

For the next eleven years Malaya ran our house with determination and devotion. Every evening I returned to a house smelling of lemon polish and a tasty dinner where each family member was served their favorite dish. Malaya was also familiar with Jewish cooking and on holidays prepared feasts for crowds. Soon, when the children needed to be chauffeured to play dates or after-school activities, we paid for her driving lessons and bought her a used car. She enjoyed traveling with us on winter ski weekends, where she would send us to the mountain with freshly baked rolls and thermoses filled with stew and hot chocolate. On these weekends, too, she did the laundry, cleaned and watched our non-skiing youngest, then joined us in our evening outings to the bowling alley or movie theater. I was the one who, concerned about spoiling our children, gave them chores and established a quota of points each had to meet in helping Malaya.

My "Domestic Goddess" had no family in the USA, but was deeply involved with her church in Brooklyn. On weekends and holidays, she stayed with fellow church members, an aging brother-sister duo. Midweek evenings in her room she spent on her own phone line on church business. Having grown up in apartheid, she basked in the absence of our family skin-color divide, yet drew her own comfort zone as an employee. She served dinner and then retired immediately to let our family eat alone, our chance to chat with the children, hear about their schools and friends, and discuss issues from gerbils and haunted castles to Judaism and presidential elections.

Malaya was talkative, and we soon learned about her fiancé who had impregnated another woman. The betrayed young Malaya lost her trust in men and never dated again. She insisted that we replace the queen-size bed in her room with a single cot. We also learned about her childhood in South Africa, growing up in a fishing village among a large family whose photographs decorated her room along with photos of Caucasian children she had raised in the over two decades prior to her living with us.

We also discovered that for her South African family, Malaya was "the rich aunt from America." She sent most of her earnings to them. The little she kept she refused to deposit in a bank because in South Africa "once, a bank went out of business and everyone lost their money." Whenever we suggested that she open a bank account where we trusted our own money, she countered with "Have you been searching my room?"

When she had first moved in with us, I took it with humor when she would say "the Hortons didn't do it this way," and expected me to follow a phantom manual of her previous employers' little daily choices. I especially made a point of not relinquishing my children's psyche to "the Hortons"—nor to Malaya. Ron and I were in sync as we navigated the complexities of marriage, careers, shared values, and the merging of two sets of children. Malaya's job was to take over the physical management of our house. It was up to us—not "the Hortons"—to set the tone.

With the burden of running the house delegated, I could focus my short early mornings and longer evening hours on quality time with my children, and the weekends on my expanded family. We played Scrabble, Boggle, Pictionary and Monopoly; we painted, embroidered, crafted, and glued; we sang silly songs, planted tomatoes, assembled giant puzzles, and picnicked; I taught the children dance moves and wove thousands of bedtime stories well into their teenage years. Yet, true to a guarantee extracted by the new magazine management after a corporate buyout, I took no time off to accompany my daughters' classes to the pumpkin farm or for Mother's Day lunches. Malaya did it. I used my sick days to attend school plays, and went to work when I was truly sick, while Malaya met the children's school bus and took them home for milk and cookies. She supervised their homework time, and Ron checked it for content.

With this backing at home, I was able to leap to the position of publisher for a prestigious women's magazine in a smaller company. I was one of only four females to hold such a business—not editorial—position in the mid-80s among the top 200 largest USA-based magazines; the two dominant companies publishing women's magazines, Hearst and Condé Nast, still assigned the running of their publications to men only. For the first time I was earning more than Malaya's salary, my pocket money, my commuting expenses—and the cost of therapy to deal with the sexual pestering of a new boss who viewed my rebuffing him as my "lack of team attitude."

Finally, pretending that motherhood was irrelevant to who I was ended. My brightest moment at my first meeting with my staff was revealing that I had children.

At that time Ron and I moved into a larger home. Malaya opted out of her ground floor bedroom in favor of designing her own suite in the windowed basement, complete with a living room and a full bath with a tub. I was not alarmed when in the new house she referred to her queendom as "her kitchen" and would not let me near "her" pots or "her" stove. As arthritis began settling in Malaya's shoulder, I budgeted in the extra cost of a weekly service to perform the heavy cleaning duties. She was still the one that called the plumber or the appliance repair service. She shopped with our credit card. She arranged play dates with mothers who made the exception for her of trusting "the help" in a suburb where no other mothers were employed outside their homes.

Since my bond with my biological daughters was sound, I viewed their attachment to their caretaker as healthy. However, as the years marched on, our household went through a slow transformation. I was the first to realize that it was a mutation, a gene gone awry in the evolution of our family cadence. While I set the rhythms and guarded our private quality time and our psychological spaces, Malaya's efficiency wove fishing nets of dependency around us. She insisted on polishing my husband's shoes and pressing his shirts; she hand-washed my sweaters. Our son, who moved back with us for graduate school, enjoyed her delicious food at all hours of the day and night. Yet her power turned to tyranny. No longer hiding behind "the Hortons," the dictates were Malaya's own. She loved the girls, but as each entered puberty, gone was the tenderness she had shown them when they were young. In the mornings, I rushed to beat her to waking them up as she would shake their legs, yank their blankets, or call out impatiently from the doorways in what we secretly called her "Gestapo voice." She fresh-squeezed my orange juice each day, but would fight with me when I straightened "her" hall coat closet. At dinnertime, instead of retiring to her room and her phone, she'd hover on the stairwell, eaves-dropping, and would break into our conversations. She snitched about one family member to another in an annoyed tone on matters that had nothing to do with her.

"An intelligent, capable woman who chose not to have her own home and family has problems we can never fully comprehend," I told Ron. "Our house and family are the center of her being; we must show her compassion."

One day, when my car needed to be repaired, I asked Malaya when it would be convenient for her to lend me hers. In response, she turned to my daughter who was having a snack at the kitchen table and said "Because of your mother you'll miss the birthday party."

"You'll never again turn my child against me," I told Malaya, my voice hard as steel. "Never."

"I quit!" Swiveling away from the stove, she flung the pan and the spatula into the sink and strode off.

I stood rooted in place, shaking with fury. The equation was clear. My children's loyalties should not be challenged in our home, the nest of their emotional safety.

An hour later, Malaya acted as if nothing had transpired. I chose to forgive.

Malaya's dream was to travel to South Africa to visit her many brothers and sisters and their children, but since they needed her money for the house they were building, she could save little. One brother and two sisters had died by the time she managed to take that trip more than twenty years after leaving South Africa. According to her report, the whole village came out to welcome her, waving the American flag. There was music and laughter. Her brothers and their broods of children—some already married and parents themselves—proudly showed her the large house they had built with her money. The love, respect, and gratitude she received were worth two decades of sacrifice.

Life went on in our household while the shifts in Malaya's internal weather systems flashed warning signals on our emotional radars and became more frequent. Malaya's cold front was closing in, angry mumbling and curt admonitions were soon followed by the eclipse of the sun—or a cyclone. One day, I returned from work to find a kitchen cabinet door hanging lopsided, deep scratches inside it and two broken drawers indicating rampage. "The drawer was stuck," she said. Although my PMS never brought wreckage, I sympathized with her menopausal mood and made no comment as I hired a carpenter.

Usually the eruption demarcated the end of the stormy weather, and calm would settle upon the house for a few months. Malaya was back to her old cheery self, and her magic wand took care of everything, lulling me into gratitude. Little by little, though, her irritability would rise, her tone would turn belligerent, and she would bad-mouth us to the chimney sweep or water meter reader.

Our teenage children would have reported any abuse, I knew, but they weren't mature enough to diagnose what I was seeing: the quiver of arrows she used to exert control.

"The dynamics in our house are sick," I told my husband. Malaya dominated the air. She was the most vocal person in our large household. She was the only one who no longer respected the space we gave one another. When she did not have her way on matters small or large, she would announce, "I quit."

How could we let go of the most indispensible person among us? Even if I didn't have a career, I would not have been the all-consuming homemaker Malaya was. I'd be out and about like my neighborhood mothers, shopping one day and returning merchandise the next, ordering takeout meals, and rising to the weekly challenge of separating the whites from the colors to wash. And having lived through many bitter experiences with incompetent, indolent, and dishonest help, I knew that I would only throw my life into complete chaos. I reminded myself that "The devil you know is better than the one you don't," and enlisted Ron in my tiptoeing around her demands and moods.

I had told Malaya many times that if she controlled her temper, she could live with us until old age. Her age, though, was an issue. When she was a child, a government official had once arrived in her remote fishing village. He listed all the children, giving them an estimated year of birth, and dating all their birthdays as July 1st. "I was two years older than my brother. Now I am two years younger," she told me. She must inform the gynecologist about this four-year mistake, I told her when she went to consult with him about her menopause. Even more important, I explained, was that she would have to work four more years before collecting Social Security benefits. It might be fixed if, on her visit to South Africa, she presented witnesses and her brother's documents, which he had since corrected. She never did.

In the years Malaya was sending money to South Africa, we advised her that the house she was paying for should be put in her name even if she would never live there. As all our financial guidance was met with resistance, so was this advice ignored. But Ron insisted we pay her on the books, get her medical insurance, and take out taxes and Social Security so she would receive benefits at retirement age.

One morning in the early 90s, I sat in the kitchen and nursed a cup of coffee in the kitchen after Ron had left for his office. I was planning a rare day of working from home; the winds of change had long ago sent me to open my own consulting firm with five offices across the country.

"Do you have enough cash for the cleaners?" I asked Malaya.

Instead of a reply, she withdrew from the drawer the wallet in which we kept money for small expenses and threw it at me.

The fight that ensued was no different from those that had taken place over the last few years when Malaya's rage peaked. It was my husband's reaction, though, when I called to report this fight that broke the pattern.

"Yes, I knew there'd be trouble when I left you alone in the kitchen with her," he told me, and a chill climbed up my spine. Not only Ron's internal barometer of Malaya's moods had predicted that the volcano was about to erupt, but that he had known that I was in the direct path of it. I also discovered that she had beaten me in reaching him to complain about me. She believed we were on equal footing when it came to claiming my husband's good will. She believed that he would side with her against me.

Had Ron and I been complicit in allowing Malaya to overstep the boundaries, or was the situation inevitable given her willfulness?

The sick dance that had taken hold of our household must be exorcised, I told Ron later. The house was hers, the kitchen was hers, my children were hers, and she did for him everything she would do for her own man since she craved no intimacy. The only problem was that I was still walking this earth. "We've gotten so used to her dominating our psyche, we don't see how pathological our dynamics have become," I said. In our combined family, we had successfully created a new universe where two sets of children fully considered themselves siblings. All six of us got along, some even spectacularly.

Nodding miserably, mumbling how he loved his starched shirts, Ron agreed that in our "Brady Bunch" family the housekeeper was no Alice. It was time to end the dictatorship.

It was October. That evening, before our hearts eased back into the routine acceptance of the dripping poison that had seeped into our collective consciousness, I wrote Malaya a long letter. Thanking her for her eleven years of service and devotion, I requested that she seek a position elsewhere. She could leave now or stay until the first of the year—her choice. Either way, she would get her large Christmas bonus, which had been our way of saving money for her. I held back from writing how her disrespect of me as a human being echoed the maltreatment I had suffered under my chauvinistic employers; that she had never been treated in our house with anything less than empathy and kindness.

Malaya chose to stay through Christmas, and our home settled into a couple of pleasant months. The soft part of our relationship restored, Malaya and I resumed our old bantering, playing with words as we imitated each other's accent. While I worked sixty hours a week, our youngest, now in high school, drove herself around, reducing Malaya's chores. At times, one of the children would ask us to reconsider the decision to let Malaya go—after all, who would cook? When I said that I would, they suggested that I might try starting small, perhaps a breakfast.... But even they didn't grasp that Malaya was my helpmate, "my wife." I was overwhelmed by what awaited me. Every bit of responsibility formerly shouldered by her would be mine to deal with.

The sacrifice was all mine. Yet, in moments when fondness and regret battled in equal measures, my indignation helped me restore my old vision of a tranquil family life and a secure home.

"We've each been through a tough divorce before," I consoled my husband as much as myself. "We came through happier. We'll get through this one, too."

In January 1993, Malaya started working for a recent widower. She moved into his posh home in Westchester county and was assigned a beautiful upstairs room, along with his late wife's BMW. Pleased with her new position, she joined the local church and soon immersed herself in that community. For the next decade, she became the gatekeeper of the widower's love life, fielding women's phone calls and giving him a piece of her mind about the ones she served her delicious dinners to. His married children discovered her culinary talents, and she delighted them with her holiday meals. She traveled with them on their vacations, caring for the host of grandchildren. And when the widower died, she moved in with one of his daughter's family.

Soon enough though, in an echo of the problems in our household, the daughter asked Malaya to live elsewhere, but retained her as a full-time day nanny. Now in her late sixties, Malaya could no longer do housework.

Since her South African house had been completed, she sent less money and saved for a second trip. She didn't want to wait twenty more years and managed to get there just a few years after her first visit. By then, her closest brother had also died. All the second generation families living in her house were busy. No one came to welcome her.

The details of the rest of this visit were never fully recounted, but there was no more talk of another trip. Nor were there any savings after a lifetime of hard work and frugal living.

In the eighteen years since Malaya had left our employment, I embraced the silence of a house emptied even of the last of my children and turned to writing fiction full-time. Malaya and I kept in loose touch. Some years we exchanged a Christmas or a birthday card. I invited her to our children's weddings.

Nevertheless, I had not expected the turn of events when my youngest daughter, now a high-powered career mother herself, called me in tears. In her mid-seventies, Malaya was sick and poor. Her eyesight partially gone, her arthritic fingers locked, Malaya was unable to find work. I called and learned that the Social Security my husband had insisted upon covered Malaya's rent of a small room in someone's suburban home, rescuing her from homelessness. Her medical bills were large and mounting. Her formerly size 14 body had shrunk to a size 8 because she had no money for food. She had no clothes to fit her new frame. And there was no one to drive her around. The new church to which she had devoted the last decade and a half to—a mixed congregation of the local wealthy Caucasians and their African-American help—did not reciprocate. Her previous Brooklyn church friends had either died, were too far away and too old, or had forgotten her in the intervening years. "I never understood how someone can end up poor and alone," my daughter said when I reported back. "Now I do."

And as I put yet another large check in the mail to Malaya and pack for her my favorite cream-colored suit that reminds me of the first time we met, I recall my years of cracking the glass ceiling while the woman who helped me became an enemy within. And I struggle with the question of why I support her so many years later, and for how long.

Independent Study

Robert King

On my desk, half a rock, one side a rough lump,
the other polished, smooth stripes of minerals,
a creamy landscape with a point of brown star
in the center—a gift from a blind student.

What had she thought she felt? Or felt she thought?
The rough and smooth in our voices as we talked?
The inside feels like marble, milk, like skin.
The outside feels like everything else in the world.

Feelings

I'd been proud of the way
   our bodies memorize our lives,
hands knowing the way keys

turn, locating the switches
   in each dark room,
but after visiting a museum

of pioneers with its pitters
   and graters, tappers and gougers,
rusted shapes I couldn't imagine the use of,

work that was second nature turned
   incomprehensible, my hands
hung like empty grapples wanting something.

Although, for that matter, my hands
   have all but forgotten
the house before this one, little

of my body enduring in the various nubs,
     knobs, handles,
I came so casually to believe in.

It makes me think there is
     no history, only one generation
of hands and then another, each of us

doing the work of the day, the day's short work.
     Even though once, by a high stream,
like grandfather's a century ago,

I gathered water loosely up to my mouth,
     a broken bowl sufficient unto itself,
an implacable knowledge that endures.

The Want of Molly

Jeffrey N. Johnson

The first night at Aunt Molly's house was not made for sleep. Though the old bungalow creaked and groaned as if it were forever settling, what kept twelve-year-old Aaron awake were his aunt's late night ramblings. Most of what passed through the plaster wall was gibberish, but he could tell by the woman's inflections that she was speaking to some imaginary friend, at times even breaking into spirited debate. On the second night, Aaron stepped into the hall and pressed an ear to her door.

"Men dig," he heard her say. "Always digging. Holes, trenches, ditches. Can't find a man without a shovel in his hand." Aaron waited nervously before knocking, then lurched back as the door swung open. "Whad you want?" his aunt said, her crimped and worried face gaping up at him. Her sleeveless nightgown wasn't much different than the rag-tag line of house dresses she wore every day, and the shallow troughs of skin under her cheeks and upper arms made it look like a great deal of fat had been sucked out of her. Standing there barefoot, toe-to-toe, Aaron noticed for the first time he had grown taller than her.

"I thought I heard you talking to someone," her nephew said, looking past her. The paisley wallpaper made Molly's bedroom vibrate, and the tiny framed pictures of hummingbirds did little to steady the space.

"You see anyone here to be talked to?"

"No ma'am."

"Then I must notta been talking to no one. Now go on. Don't you sleep?"

The boy went back to the guestroom. It would take several more nights of Molly's fidgety tonic of gossip and gab before the house attained a regularity worth sleeping to. The only thing in Molly's room to converse with was a bright-eyed doll peering from a wicker crib, the same crib in which Molly had been laid after her birth forty-seven years ago. Despite a difficult delivery and the uncertain days that followed, she had slept in that same bedroom ever since. It was rumored that Molly was deprived of oxygen for a moment too long. Others figured her problems began at conception.

Aaron's grandfather had bequeathed the old bungalow in town to Molly out of fear of what might become of her. Though Aaron's father was annoyed at the patrimonial slight, his mother didn't seem to mind as she likely feared for her older sister in the same way. She didn't drive, never held a job, and was shaky at best when confronted with multiple choices. The house was within walking distance of the market, the bank, and the post office, which satisfied most of Molly's needs.

Aaron's parents lived three miles out of town on a one acre parcel surrounded by the more weighty farms of the Virginia Piedmont. Demanding both the daily rigor of the urban and the spiritual borderlands of the rural, his father drove forty miles into Washington, D.C. each day to sit behind a government desk and dream of his weekends in the country. The summer Aaron's mother decided to rejoin the workforce, sharing the long commute with her husband to the Patent Office, it was decided that Aaron would be dropped off at his aunt's house each Monday morning to spend the week. The boy fought the idea, claiming he was too old for a babysitter. He didn't admit to being slightly afraid of Molly. He wasn't sure what to make of her. Aaron's mother, grasping for justification, claimed that Aunt Molly was the best thing for a boy Aaron's age. Molly could be a second mother to him, she said, though the way she avoided eye contact left her son in doubt.

Aaron assumed Aunt Molly was considered "motherly" because she baked. His own mother had trouble finding the bakery counter in the grocery store, but Molly baked like a woman obsessed. It was her only talent and the one thing she handled with grace. Her house was always filled with the smell of warm bread, cakes, and pastries, most of which were destined for the local market and provided her only trickle of income. A rooster egg timer on the window sill was always diligently set so she wouldn't ruin the sweet-smelling house with the stink of burnt dough and fouled confectionery. Each morning for breakfast she treated Aaron to fresh rye or pumpernickel with elderberry preserves, and throughout the day she fed him treats that his mother would hardly have approved of. In this way, over the first few weeks of summer, Aaron's fear of his aunt waned and morphed into something resembling love.

The house in town was frozen in time from the lean years of their ancestors. Molly was both archivist and housekeeper, a conservator with a dust mop. Though the curtains were threaded from the sun and the ancient lace doilies were dry-rotting on the arms of overstuffed chairs, every flat surface in the house could pass the white-glove test. For Aaron, the house was a history lesson on life in mid-twentieth century America. He listened to dusty 78s of Hank Williams and George Jones on the record phonograph, held his ear to the gothic radio that broadcast only faint winnowy static, and skimmed the library of *Life Magazines* and faceless *National Geographics*.

One day Molly came across Aaron lying on the floor with his nose in an issue of *Life*, studying the Zapruder series of the Kennedy assassination with a magnifying glass. Molly stood over him as he examined each frame with eager eyes, searching for pieces of the president's brain exploding across the image. There was no way to sanitize something so public and violent from the innocent eyes of a twelve-year-old boy. Aaron wondered about the president's last thought as the bullet passed through his head, and what sensation, if any, he might have felt. He wondered the same of the president's wife as she climbed frantically over the trunk of the limo. The killing was suddenly very real to Aaron and provided an excitement he hadn't known before.

Molly said, "They done got him good, didn't they." The boy looked over his shoulder and saw her there in the same kind of lazy house dress she wore every day.

"Do you remember it?" Aaron asked.

"Wasn't but a dozen years ago. Lost his head the same month your momma birthed you." She started back to the kitchen to inspect an oven full of rising banana bread. "Guess it all evened out," she added, trailing off.

She had a closet full of those smock-like dresses, and Aaron wondered if it wasn't by design they resembled nightgowns. Several times each day he would find her dozing, sitting upright on either the sofa or the splintery porch swing where she waited for the rooster egg timer to wake her. The way her shoulders dipped and mouth hung open made her look like she'd given up on a part of her life. But what made her naps unsettling was that she slept with her eyes open, with always a spooked gaze, as if she were trying to penetrate some other dimension.

Aaron spent most afternoons that summer with his friend Mitch Harris, either tooling around the back alleys of town or trespassing up and down the Cole Creek Valley. They spent the long summer days hardening their lungs with stolen cigarettes, lighting things on fire to see how they burned, and inventing other games of questionable legality. Mitch's father owned a used car dealership in the county seat, and was as known for making deals as for sleeping with the long line of secretaries that had worked under his predatory gaze. Aaron knew Mitch was afraid of his father, as he'd witnessed the man's two personas and how it was impossible to predict which one would show up—the one who tried to ingratiate himself with the local boys by telling foul-mouth jokes, some of which the youngsters didn't fully understand, or the one who would greet Mitch with a violent backhand across the face. Mitch's mother, a waifish soul possessing no more kindness than meanness, busied herself corralling Mitch's three younger siblings and cashing her husband's checks. She was partial to the ease of low expectations, and her eldest son was happy to accommodate her.

Aaron and Mitch's favorite pastime was tormenting the town bum. They found him one day loitering on the corner of Westbury and Chapel, wearing a nylon ski cap turned up over the brow and a surplus camouflage overcoat that was several sizes too large. Mitch had brought a pocket full of dried up horse turds from a farmer's field (he was handy that way), and chucked one at the bum, thumping him upside the head. The man's reaction was subdued, his speech mottled as if he had no tongue, though it was there in plain sight, resting on his lower lip like a raw hamburger patty. He came at them slow and clumsy, his face down as if forced to plan each step. His stride was like that of a naked man running over sharp rocks.

Mitch yelled, "Incoming!" and released a barrage of turds into the air. The boys peed their pants as they ran away.

The bum's proper name was Aubrey, but anyone who called him anything called him Mumbles. The town's inhabitants referred to him as "our bum," not out of any sense of indentured servitude or that he somehow belonged to them, but that he had earned a place in the community, a tolerated place where he wasn't perceived as a threat. Or perhaps it was just a way to say that the position of town bum was occupied and there was no room for another. So long as he was *their* bum, their *only* bum, Mumble's position was secure and the town accepted him with a steady endurance, like it would a leaning lamp post or a root-cracked sidewalk. No one seemed to know where Aubrey came from, and it was doubtful anyone could have understood him had he offered up the information. One could only guess his age. Some said he was about fifty, but this number didn't fit with the older folks in town who said he had always been there, like the grain elevator or the railroad. Whatever the number, the years did not play well on him.

Aubrey fished Cole Creek every day for anything that was biting, usually catfish or smallmouth bass, but in the lengthening drought that summer his prey settled downstream in the warm brown backwater of the Cawhauler Dam. It was too far to walk, especially through the dense brush and thickets on the creek's muddy banks, so Aubrey was more dependent than usual on the generosity of the townsfolk. The local grocer, to whom Molly sold her baked goods, always left a handful of slightly expired fruit or vegetables in the alley next to the dumpster, and those in town who occasionally hired Aubrey for odd jobs around their yards (never inside) were inclined to prepare him a bag lunch.

When Aunt Molly informed Aaron she'd hired Mumbles to paint her house and that he was expected to help, Aaron was suffused in a preteen windstorm of dread and embarrassment. Like all young boys at one time or another, he wanted to flee, to break from the threat of shame and responsibility, and leave town with all his belongings tied to the end of a stick. Then he whiplashed to the other extreme and promised to paint the whole house by himself.

Molly shoveled off a dozen oatmeal-raisin cookies from her baking sheet, shaking her head. "You can't paint the whole house. You're too small."

"I am not. I promise I'll do it."

"I'm gonna buy two of everything. Two scrapers, two brushes, and two'a dem funny painter hats."

"Then I got stuff I gotta do," Aaron pleaded, almost in tears.

She waved her spatula at him.

"You ain't got no stuff that I can see."

The torments of Mumbles were a constant that summer, and Aaron began assembling a time line of the minor atrocities he and Mitch had inflicted on him. Only the day before, Mitch had hit the poor bum square in the back with a water balloon, and by the time Mumbles turned around, Mitch was long gone, leaving Aaron doubled over and giggling in his wake. Mitch never said what he was going to do next, or when, and now Aaron, who was usually little more than an accomplice, was growing wary of his friend's casual cruelty.

The next day Aaron escorted his aunt arm-in-arm to the paint store where she pestered the manager for an hour over brush types, rollers, cleaning agents, and an infinite array of color samples. Molly was not good with choices. The next afternoon, a delivery truck pulled up to her house and a man unloaded a canvas drop-cloth, two scrapers, two wide synthetic brushes, two cans of turpentine, ten gallons of primer, and another ten gallons of flat white paint onto her porch. Molly signed the receipt by making her mark, a scribbly "M" that could have been read as a "W." The delivery man carried his clipboard back to the truck, shaking his head.

When Aubrey came to Molly's house that first morning in mid-July, he lingered on the back porch for an hour without knocking. Aaron, still in his pajamas, peeked from the upstairs bedroom and saw him coming up the lawn, then burrowed back under the covers and played dead, dreading the first awkward encounter and fearing the bum might smack him at first sight.

After a while the boy thought Aubrey might have left, perhaps after seeing all the work that was going to be required. The house was peeling badly, right down to the bare wood, but it was not likely Mumbles was intimidated as he was sometimes hired by the local farmers to do some of the foulest jobs in the valley. No one in the county shoveled shit so well and without protest, and had anyone else crawled under a sty with the droppings and doodies of five thousand chickens, they might have eagerly shot themselves in the head the same evening. But Mumbles always worked dutifully and without complaint. It's doubtful a little peeling paint even phased him. The more likely reason he loitered on Molly's porch that morning was the smell of her early batch of bread still raising its tender crown, seeping through the windows and circling the house like a warm embrace. It was doubtful Aubrey was used to such things, though it might have reminded him of an earlier time.

Molly eventually found Aubrey when she went out to hang laundry. She hollered for Aaron, who lumbered out in his pajama bottoms, thinking he might be less likely to be struck if only half clothed. To his surprise, Mumbles regarded him as he would a pumpkin or a bush. At first the boy thought he was being shunned, but then noticed the dirty man was staring at his aunt in a kind of befuddled longing. The only hint of emotion was in his eyes as he took in the chattering woman and the smell from her oven. Aunt Molly seemed oblivious to his gaze and went about giving painfully long and incoherent instructions of how she wanted the house painted. Then without warning, Aubrey broke from his trance, picked up a shiny new scraper, and went to work on a short section of wall by the chimney. Molly rambled on for another minute before shooing Aaron off to get dressed and fed. Before going inside, she pondered her help for a moment, watching him scrape hard on the first board. "I'm going to bake you a cake," she exclaimed, before tromping off to the kitchen.

Aaron stalled as long as he could before taking his place on the other side of the chimney. Together he and Aubrey worked the short end of the house, shearing the dry chips of paint off the clapboard in white explosions under the ring of the metallic scrapers. The boy neglected the areas of paint that clung stubbornly to the siding, but Aubrey had a different approach, working methodically, scraping only one board at a time and refusing to move on until there was nothing left but the chalky wood grain. He was slow but thorough. They worked together those first few weeks with the chimney separating them, giving Aaron time and space to acclimate to his strange new workmate. Once they turned the corner, they worked side-by-side over the hatch to the cellar as Aaron watched Aubrey's puffy hands scrape away the generations. Not once did they speak, though in time they worked together like old friends who were no longer embarrassed by silence. Aubrey came and went on his own schedule, usually working for several hours each morning and leaving only after Molly had set him up with a bag of sandwiches and cookies. Then he would take his lunch and disappear into the valley to fish and sleep under the sycamores, dreaming his unimaginable dreams.

The land was owned by the railroad and the barn was surplus property long forgotten by the Norfolk Southern. Railroad ties smelling thick of creosote were stacked unevenly against the barn and scattered around the yard among pieces of rusty equipment that were past their useful lives. Mitch rattled the padlock on the front door of the barn, but the metal had long since fused together. On the back side, away from the rails and behind a thicket of briars, he spotted the top half of a Dutch door, and it didn't take him long to find the trampled path burrowing under the bramble to the door's base. The two friends crawled on their hands and knees, and when they reached the bottom half of the door, they pulled it open and felt the cool mildewy air touch their faces.

Once inside, Mitch kicked along like he had been there many times before, but to Aaron this felt like a home invasion, no different from prowling inside a neighbor's house. He took silent steps as he acclimated to the light, feeling his way along the hay dust and compacted earth. He was afraid to move anything or to leave even a trace that he had been there. Mitch swaggered ahead, inspecting the line of abandoned stalls until he came to one where the straw had been brushed aside and the dirt floor swept clear. On one side, organized neatly on a wooden crate, was a bum's kitchen: stacked cans of Sterno, matches, a crusted frying pan and boiling pot, plastic bags of half-eaten baked goods, and a plastic tray containing a bent fork, a spoon, and several kinds of dull knives. Inside the crate were expired cans of cream corn, string beans, and a near empty bottle of Mad Dog 20/20. Mitch hopped over the gate.

Aaron was taken by Mitch's profile. There was some new twist to his face, something resembling hate.

Mitch stared down at the little pantry. "This is pathetic," he said. Before Aaron could see what he had found, Mitch kicked the crate and sent the cans, pots, and utensils strewing across the stall. He stomped on a can of cream corn as Aaron climbed onto the gate.

"Stop it," Aaron said, jumping down to the hard-pack. He recognized the bread bags as the ones his aunt used.

Mitch walked across the stall, picked up a dented can of Sterno, and put it in his pocket. "What a loser," he said. In the next stall he found a woolen nest of blankets over a thick bed of straw. Above were several more threaded covers folded neatly in the hayloft. Somewhere between rage and glee, Mitch jumped the fence and went about wrecking Aubrey's bed. He stomped and twisted in a kind of epileptic dance before kicking the crap out of the bedding, sending wads of moldy blanket and straw in all directions. He didn't stop until Aaron caught him off balance and shoved him to the ground.

"Knock it off," Aaron cried.

Mitch fell against the feed stall where his hand went through the collar and came down on something tin and hollow. Instead of taking a swing at Aaron, he rolled onto his knees and reached into the trough where he retrieved a metal tin with a marlin on the cover. His face turned greedy as he placed it in the middle of Aubrey's wrecked bed and flipped off the top.

"Put it back," Aaron told him. "It's his stuff."

Like a conquistador searching for gold with the tip of his sword, Mitch started tossing things out of the box with no more than a cursory inspection, passing on the few things in the poor man's life that might have value to him: a deck of cards, a metal button, rusty fishing hooks, seashell fossils, a dozen foil gum wrappers, a perfectly shaped acorn, a mercury dime. At the bottom were two pages torn from an early *Playboy Magazine*, and Mitch quickly stuffed them in his pocket. Then they saw the photograph. Lying in the bottom of the desecrated tin was a small black and white of a young woman, and it took them a few seconds to recognize who it was.

"That's your aunt." Mitch said.

"It is not," Aaron countered, not quite believing himself.

"Mumbles is laying your aunt!"

Aaron wanted to punch the bastard. "She is not!" he yelled back. "She just feeds him."

"Uncle Mumbles."

"Screw you."

Aaron took a swing, but Mitch had been so toughened by his father's backhands that Aaron's unimpressive fist made little impression. That wasn't their first fight that summer, as they were in that childish he-man mode of fighting over just about anything, but this one struck Aaron as worth fighting for. The presence of Molly's photo among the bum's trinkets stunned even his feeble preteen reasoning. Though Mitch had proven nothing, his accusation had a ring of truth to it. As Aaron lie on his back shielding Mitch's overhand blows, his mind focused on the image of his aunt. The photo had a serrated edge that was popular in the fifties and was of Molly in the spring of her adult years. She had the same bewildered face, but looked vaguely pretty in a way her nephew had never imagined. Her eyes still had that restless quality, but her gaze showed greater interest in life and whatever was in front of her, a kind of interest Aaron had never before seen in her. If Molly had ever loved, this photo might have captured that brief magical time.

At first he thought Aubrey might have snuck inside his aunt's house and stolen the photo, but he quickly dismissed the idea as he couldn't see the man doing anything subversive. He also knew that his aunt, ever concerned for her privacy, would never let a man into her house, especially a man like Aubrey. People would talk. It wouldn't be proper. Though there was never a hint that Molly and Aubrey had known each other in their youth, there was no evidence to show they hadn't. The only other theory was that Molly had given Aubrey the photo.

Aaron slept on a sofa bed in the upstairs sitting room next to a bookcase lined with the brittle spines of old hardbacks: *A Tree Grows in Brooklyn*, *Migratory Birds of the East Coast*, and *The First Thanksgiving*. The only interesting part of the room was what came through the walls on a nightly basis, and now his aunt's jabbering was coming later each evening in ever-rising distress. She had changed the delivery schedule of her baked goods from morning to evening, wheeling her cart the three blocks to the back of Caldwell's grocery near closing time, and each evening she came home a little later. She claimed it was the only cool part of the day for her to walk and get her exercise. The night Aaron heard her flat-footed steps come through the back door at eleven-thirty, he placed a milk glass against the wall and waited for Molly to close her bedroom door.

"Men beg," her muffled voice carried. "Always beggin'. Beggin' them things ain't proper." She paused, and this time Aaron could hear her labored breathing. "One track mind, I tell you." The floor creaked under her nervous pacing. "Can't be doing that. No, sir. Not proper." Her voice was shrill, and caused in Aaron a rising anxiety as he pressed his ear into the glass.

Three square windows were lined up across the long side of the barn, and the lamplight from inside glowed brightest from the center. The night was black, but for the red and green lights on the nearby switching tower. The air was so thick with humidity it choked out all but the brightest stars. The boys stood tiptoe on the poorly stacked railroad ties that wobbled beneath their feet, and they gripped the window trim with straining fingers. Inside, the light from a kerosene lamp made the horizontal boards of the stall glow yellow, while the rest of the space receded in varying shades of darkness, like a chapel lit in solemn Mass. The two boys looked down and saw them there on the rebuilt bedding. She was spread out on her back like she'd fallen from a great height. The loose jiggling flesh of her arms and legs were all of her they could see as he was on top, his hunched and hairy back pushing between her legs in a kind of hemorrhage and making a sound like Aaron had once heard from the walrus tank at the zoo. Their bodies were all tensed up and flabby at the same time. Like some instinctive animal, Aubrey never stopped his manic attack, pounding ever harder into the flabby frame of Molly. Aaron was afraid he might break her, and was absorbed in shame and confusion as the sound of the katydids merged with the thrusting of Mumbles. His grip on the window sill loosened from the shock of what he was seeing.

"Holy crap," Mitch said. As he pressed his nose on the glass, the stack of ties shifted and sent the boys tumbling to the ground. They scraped and bloodied their shins and forearms, but felt little as they jumped up and ran down the tracks toward town. Mitch followed him up the street laughing hysterically, while Aaron was near tears.

"Go home," Aaron said. "Stop following me."

"I want something to eat."

"Beat it!"

Mitch kept after him, perhaps knowing he would get his way. They ended up on Molly's back porch munching from a tin of molasses cookies. Mitch examined his wounds as Aaron stared quietly across the yard.

"So has he been here?" Mitch asked. "In her bedroom?"

"No. I'da heard them."

"She must want it bad to do it with Mumbles."

"What do *you* know about girls?"

"As much as you, shit-for-brains." Mitch noticed the paint cans, then motioned toward the brushes soaking in a mason jar filled with spirits.

"What's that stuff?" he asked.

The usual August drought settled on the Piedmont, counting thirty days since the last rain. Yards were chapped and brown with only weeds seeming to thrive, and the ground had shrunken back from the sidewalks leaving gaps wide enough for mice to crawl through. The whole state was a tinderbox, so it was no surprise when one Saturday morning the valley caught fire.

It started near town on the shallow side of the tracks where the tall brush lay on its side. The flames spread up the valley to the northeast where they devoured fifty acres of pasture, four barns, two resident thoroughbreds, and the house of Bill and Mandy Picket. The fire chief was the first to find the charred remains of Mandy and her infant daughter in the room where they had been napping.

The first thing that had burned was the abandoned barn near the tracks, where the piles of creosote soaked railroad ties smoldered for two days. All that was left of the barn was the cinder block foundation. Nearby lay an empty gallon tin of turpentine and a can of Sterno.

Molly was asleep on the sofa when the sheriff knocked on her back door. She dawdled to the door where she found the uniformed man looking over her paint supplies. The air outside was tinted with a residue of smoke and stink that made Molly raise her nose and grimace. She stood there wringing her hands in her apron, blinking those eyes that never rested, while the sheriff studied the label and batch number of the can of turpentine.

"Miss Blount," he said, still squinting at the can, "I'm Sheriff Clayton."

"I see who you are. You think I'm blind?"

"No ma'am, I'm sure you can see just fine." He looked up and regarded her like he would a child. "I understand you hired Aubrey Koop to paint your house."

"He does. He paints my house." She crimped her nose. "What's that stink?"

"Has he been by today?"

"He ain't got no schedule. He comes when he wants."

"Then you haven't seen him today?"

"I ain't seen no one but you snooping round my porch."

The sheriff touched the brim of his hat and stepped into the grass before turning back. "I hope you don't mind, but I'll need to borrow this." He held up the can of solvent.

"I paid good money for that."

"I understand. I'll reimburse you myself if I have to. Now, you'll call me if Aubrey shows up, won't you?"

"I might."

"Miss Blount, it's important I talk to him. I need to find him before someone else does."

The sheriff walked back to his car, leaving Molly tasting the acrid air and muttering to herself. "Men take," she said, wriggling her nose. "Always taking."

Aaron was home with his parents the weekend of the fire and over-heard his father on the phone. When told about the Picket family, his father let out a groan and shook his head. Then he spoke Aubrey's name and shook his head again. After hanging up, Aaron asked him what happened.

"There was a terrible fire near town," his father said, and then explained about the Pickets. "That's all we know."

"Was Aubrey hurt?"

His father paused and looked into his mother's stricken face.

"He doesn't seem to be around to ask."

Aaron telephoned Mitch, but his family was busy packing the car for a two-week vacation to Virginia Beach. Mitch said he'd seen the fire up close, but was hesitant to give much detail. It was old news to him now, and he didn't want to talk about it. But there was something more in his voice, a kind of nervous urgency to get off the phone and get out of town. His father could be heard yelling in the background, hurling beach chairs and insults, and Aaron was soon left with a dial tone.

The boy was anxious to be dropped off at his aunt's house Monday morning so he could walk the valley, see the destruction, and feel the place where people had died. He dropped his things at Molly's house and ran back out with such excitement that he didn't notice his aunt sitting at the dining room table, a place where she never sat. She didn't say hello or goodbye, and never offered breakfast. Aaron ran out the door without even noticing her idle kitchen.

The boy crossed the tracks and stopped on the rise where he surveyed the charred corner of the valley. The pungent air infected his nostrils as he stepped into the burnt grasses. Through the blackened sticks of the cedars, he spotted the foundation of the barn, its cinder block imprint cordoned off with yellow police tape. The piles of ties were still giving off a whither of whitish smoke. Any evidence of the origin of the blaze had been removed to the sheriff's office. He walked a few hundred yards across the ashen landscape and came to the skeletal remains of the Picket's house. He tried to imagine these two people he did not know burning like sacrifices in the marauding flames, the warmth of their home turning into some fantastic funeral pyre. He wondered if either Mandy or her daughter had woken, and he wondered about their last thoughts, or if they had had any thoughts at all. For Aaron there was an odd thrill of being there, the thrill of seeing tragedy and trying to understand without actually having to suffer for it.

When he got back to his aunt's house the door was locked, and he had to use his key for the first time to get in. Molly was back on the couch in her usual wide-eyed sleeping pose, but he could tell she was not asleep. Her eyes showed great concentration, as if she were trying to levitate something before her. Then he noticed the house's lack of bakery appeal, and he knew something was wrong.

"Aunt Molly," he said, approaching cautiously from one side. "Are you okay?"

"Whad you want?" she answered, still staring ahead.

"Has Aubrey been by?"

"Hush yourself. Can't you be quiet?" She turned her hands over and back again. "Boy's always asking questions."

Aaron backed away. "I'm gonna get some breakfast."

Some alarm seemed to go off in Molly's head, and she rushed to the kitchen, giving him a chill as she brushed past.

"Get yourself outta my kitchen. I'm feeding you. You just wait. Can't you wait?" She scrambled around the counters in a desperate huff, dropping an odd mix of things from the cabinets that satisfied no single recipe. Aaron went to the next room to watch the black and white TV and tried to block out his aunt's manic and pointless racket. An hour later he found her back on the porch swing, though she was not swinging. She seemed afraid to move, as if any motion might attract unwanted attention. Her usually orderly kitchen was now a flower dusted confusion of mixing bowls, pans, and spilled cooking oils. Aaron made himself a bowl of cereal and snatched a handful of cookies, and did the same for dinner as he left his aunt to her thoughts. He was scared for her and considered calling his mother for help, but decided instead to respect his aunt's privacy.

He waited that evening for her mottled speech through the wall, hoping to learn what was wrong, but she never came to bed. All he heard was her pacing the floor below. When the back door slammed shut, he went to the window and lifted the screen. Directly below he could see her in the shadows coming around the side of the house. She worked the padlock on the hatch to the cellar, heaved open the door, and began speaking into the hole as if having one of her bedroom conversations. But this time a voice spoke back—a series of pathetic grunts waxing from the blackness.

Aaron rushed downstairs, slid out the back door, and tiptoed across the porch. He didn't know what he was going to do. He just felt like he should be there for them. As he came to the overgrown boxwoods at the corner of the house, three beams of light flashed across the lawn from different directions and heavy footsteps tromped up the driveway and rustled through the hedgerow of the neighbor's lot. Aaron dropped to his knees and pressed into the bushes as Molly spun around and let out a shriek. A hand clasped over her mouth as two other men lit the cellar and found their prey. They pulled Aubrey from the abyss by his arms and hair, and he cowered under their blows like he'd been beaten many times in his life. Molly kicked hard to break away, but the man held her steady. His large hand covered most of her face, and fallen threads of hair obscured her eyes. He told the others to stop beating Aubrey, that there was no time for that now, as he led Molly past the boxwoods to the back door and forced her inside. Aaron's body was all seized up as he listened to the men talking.

"We shoulda waited till that crazy woman went to bed," one man said.

"I told you she had the key. Now keep him quiet."

One of the men wrapped a piece of clothes line around Aubrey's face, cinching it through his mouth. The bum huddled on his knees with a wet stain on his crotch and drool running down his chin, bracing for the next blow. Aaron heard the door close behind him and the man who had escorted Molly inside flashed a beam of light once over his head. A car came up the street with its headlights off, and as it pulled into the driveway all three men dragged Aubrey over and heaved him into the back seat. Aaron recognized the driver's face under the burning dome light as a schoolmate's father whose surname was Picket. The car and its band of men quietly rolled away.

Aaron stayed on his hands and knees under the boxwood trembling uncontrollably, trying to squeeze down the fear, but he kept replaying the scene over and over, frame-by-frame. It was not a thrill, but a quiet terror. Afraid to leave the safety of his burrow, afraid more men might be watching and waiting, he considered staying there all night. He even thought of walking the three miles of dark highway to his parent's house. He finally crawled out from the brush and crept onto the back porch where he peeked through the window. Molly was sitting on the kitchen floor with her back to the cabinets, her cheek pressed awkwardly against one shoulder. Her eyes were barely open, and the erratic spirit that once shone from them had dimmed. Aaron tried the door, but it was locked. He swallowed hard and tapped on the window.

"Aunt Molly." His breath fogged a little patch on the glass. "It's me. Can you open the door?" He rapped a little harder. "Can you please open the door?"

The newspaper said Aubrey drowned in six inches of water. That was all the drought left in Cole Creek that August, the rest having drained off toward the Chesapeake or evaporated into the very air the towns-folk breathed. He had apparently slipped on a rock and taken a bad blow to the head. There was no mention of a funeral. It was as if he'd just moved on to another town and became someone else's bum. Only years later did Aaron wonder where people like Aubrey were laid to rest.

The night of Aubrey's death was the last Aaron spent at his aunt's house. Aunt Molly, he was told, was suddenly too busy to handle him. Her needs had changed, though he knew she had lost her head.

Molly spent two months in the state mental hospital and suffered a series of "treatments" that were never fully revealed to Aaron. When she was finally allowed to go home, she was incapable of speech and was still prone to bouts of violent shaking and paranoia. From then on, Molly would see only Aaron's mother. She filed Molly's disability papers, brought her groceries, filled her many prescriptions, hired a lawn service, and convinced the Post Master to walk the two blocks and hand-deliver the mail. She made sure all of Molly's needs were cared for, though her wants were not apparent. Molly no longer had the drive to spend her days baking. Her dutiful sister, likely exhausted by her new responsibilities, simply blamed it on the new medications.

Aaron kept his promise to his aunt to paint her house, though he did so slowly, coming the next four summers by bike and eventually by car to do small sections at a time, each in the thorough and tedious way he had learned from watching Aubrey's swollen hands do their work. Not once did Molly greet him. But though the blinds were always drawn, he frequently felt watched, and a few times he caught Molly's wide eye peering from behind a pinch of drapery. That was as close to her as he could get.

When he finally finished painting the house, Aaron felt pride in what he had done—caring for his ailing aunt, paying homage to a homeless man, and adding his own generational layer to the old bungalow—though this pride was suffused with the guilt of having done nothing to help Molly and her late beau on the night of the kidnapping. And now that guilt was all the more bitter as he looked closely at the wall by the chimney where he and Aubrey had first worked side-by-side. The paint was beginning to peel.

Against his mother's wishes, Aaron decided to see his Aunt again face-to-face, to get her attention and tell her how sorry he was for what had happened and how he missed her strange ways. He went to her house at an odd hour and caught her outside, though still out of sight of the townsfolk, sitting on the back porch staring blankly at pictures in an old magazine. When she saw the front end of Aaron's car nose into the backyard, she jumped up and scurried into the house with her smock trailing behind her. The floor boards of the old porch creaked under Aaron's feet as he came to the door. He knocked and called her name, but heard only her footsteps trailing off somewhere deep inside, somewhere to rest, perhaps, and close her eyes.

In Ice, First Understanding

Angie Macri

In all the ice, I was the flame
around my baby. Her first
Christmas flared with breaking
power lines as loblolly pines
crashed, splashing air with crazed

energy. At my breast, her wet
lips breathed fallen degrees
in trees' creaking in steep
north winds. Fire fed no warmth,
and new toys hit unseen feet

in dimness with idle songs.
I was trying, and she didn't cry,
even with diapers changed
at thirty-five and my breath
petrified above her.

Such open eyes, hers, in oaken cold,
holding folds of brown like turned
earth unlocked for seed. I told

her stories to keep her close, of groaning
hulls of boats cutting oceans' roaring.

Underneath trust, under the dust
of new snow and sudden understanding,
she pulled up to stand alone for
the first time. Above us, the upper
crust of sky must have been crumbling.

Who Knows

Kristi Garboushian

Maybe my heart will open
during this intrusion.

I find your violence beyond
disorder, the spectacular trigger
you see as consecrate
flesh, your own body
functioning inward, your blood
hearing-impaired.

How angry you are,
how old
it has made you, a disaster of wrinkles,
frozen rain etched into the sky.

Nonni

Nonni,

the modification of the truth
found you beautiful—
postcards filled the space
behind your right eye

where the piano was strange
and words
were written to be read on paper.

You know the palm
in your throat
reaching to shake the rug,

you know the truth, running
parallel to earth,
teal skirt with the nylon
slip a jellyfish,

billowed and black polka-
dotted, trailed by long tentacles.
Hair in the same curled locks
worn by witches and heretics.

Louisville, KY, USA

Ellen Birkett Morris

Sex is always better in exotic places—
Italy, even Budapest, in a canopy bed
in a rented room, overlooking the sea.
But I turn to you in our familiar bed,
warm with Saturday sleep. Touch
my cheek to your gray chest hair. See
the wrinkles around your eyes. Hear
the dog begin to bark. Feel
the pulling of desire.
As the mailman rings the doorbell,
we lie together slowing.

Christmas Vandals Still at Large

Paul Crenshaw

It's almost a week now after Christmas, and the vandals who wreaked such bountiful Yuletide havoc on various nativity scenes, Christmas lights, and neighborhood vegetation in our community still have not been caught.

Last night was the third time they have struck since Christmas. When Alma George woke this morning, Jesus had no head.

"I didn't know what had happened at first," she said. "But I knew something wasn't right. It wasn't until I saw my poor baby Jesus' head half-frozen in the birdbath that I knew what they'd done. I screamed then, screamed for the Lord to do unto them as they had done unto my Jesus. But then after a while I screamed 'Lord, forgive them for they know not what they do'. Because it's Christmas and everything."

Other citizens do not share Mrs. George's capacity for forgiveness. Beula Givens, Mrs. George's next door neighbor, says she woke up to the screech of tires and grabbed a shotgun.

"I knew it was them," she told police afterward. "And I was going to kill them for what they done to Santa [referring to the defamation of a giant Santa outside the elementary school, on which a giant penis had been drawn with permanent magic marker]. I didn't even know then what they done to Jesus. Santa is bad enough, but Jesus is worse."

Mrs. Givens, who retired last year after almost thirty years of service in the public schools, stated, "But they was already gone before I could get there. Still, I fired up into the air to let them know I mean business."

The shot woke neighbor Ralph Wint, who thought he was having a heart attack.

"Turns out it was just indigestion," Wint said, relieved. Wint, who landed on Normandy Beach on June 6th, 1944, and whose grandchildren are sick and tired of hearing about it, says that he wakes almost every night with indigestion. Sometimes there is diarrhea as well, and sometimes it is so bad he goes in his pants before he can get to the bathroom, but, Wint says, he will not wear adult undergarments.

"I fought in the war," Wint said vehemently. "I'm not wearing a damn diaper."

Also in Mrs. George's nativity scene, Mary and Joseph had been doodled on, and empty beer cans littered the manger.

"It's a crying shame," Tommy Green said as he was walking his dog, a pit bull named Rosco that once chewed the legs off a neighbor's pet rabbit, past Mrs. George's house the next day.

So far to date the vandals have torn down all the Christmas lights from West 6th Street to the elementary school, chopped down a beautiful Colorado blue spruce in Carol Farris's front yard, defecated on the Methodist Church steps, drawn a giant penis on Santa Claus, and added heavy, swinging breasts to both Mary and Joseph, as well as hacking off Jesus' head.

"We're trying everything we know of to do," Sheriff John Maynor said when reached for comment, although he would not state exactly what "everything we know of to do" meant. "We're out there every night. We'll get them, if they keep doing it."

Other citizens do not share such confidence. Floyd Holt, who lives across the street from the Methodist Church, is one of them.

"He ain't even said nothing about the Baptists," Floyd was overheard saying down at the Bearcat Cafe very early the next morning. He looked worn out and smelled like bologna. "Nobody pooped on their steps. I'll bet it was one of them done it." He looked around the table, but the other four or five men looked at the walls, and no one joined him.

"Anyway, I wouldn't trust him [the Sheriff] as far as I could throw him. I know for a fact that he voted for Walter Mondale and Geraldine Ferraro."

When reached for comment about whether or not he had voted Mondale-Ferraro, Sheriff Maynor said only, "That was a long time ago."

About Holt, he said, "I once arrested him for DWI. I know he hates me because of it, but the man couldn't stand up, and he was driving around town at noon. There were children around. I had to take him in. He kept talking about some football game."

"That's bullcrap," Holt said. "I was sober as a judge."

Judge Thomas was unavailable for comment.

Police believe there may be more than one suspect, or groups of suspects.

"They've covered a lot of territory," Sheriff Maynor's deputy, Jim Higgins, who once returned a kickoff ninety-seven yards before it was called back because his best friend, Floyd Holt, had clipped, said. "Even for a small town, they've covered a lot of territory."

Last night, the deputy stated, he had driven through town turning off the Christmas lights that decorate the telephone poles along Main Street. Around one a.m. the sheriff had driven past the empty building that used to be Givens' grocery store before Kenneth Givens shot himself in the face, and is now sometimes prey to vandals and the homeless, but, as he stated, everything was fine. Just after one, he responded to a one-vehicle accident out on Highway 23 and, when he came back to town around two, all the lights had been turned back on.

"It's the damndest thing," he went on to say. "Some nights they're tearing [stuff] down; other nights they're turning the lights back on."

"I agree it's a terrible thing," Mayor Williams stated, for the record. "But I'll bet you a hundred dollars it's some kids messing around. I don't think it's the end of the world."

When asked what he thought about someone cutting Jesus' head off, the Mayor would not answer directly.

"Don't print this," he told me, "But some people in this town get a little too serious about their religion."

Shawn Wint, a senior at Hooks High and grandson of Ralph Wint, when hearing of the mayor's comments about kids being the perpetrators said, "Whatever, man. He doesn't know."

Wint, who once peed on his grandfather's service uniform because he was sick and tired of hearing about D-Day, is flunking out of high school, although he has not told his parents. Mrs. Farris, who teaches senior English and whose Colorado blue spruce was chopped down, thinks Shawn can still graduate, but no one else shares her optimism.

"He's not a bad kid," Mrs. Farris said.

"She should concentrate on the kids who actually have a chance," Principal Lassiter said of Mrs. Farris. "But you can't tell her that. You can't say 'This kid has no chance'. I don't know why, but you can't."

"She's a cunt," Wint said. "A goody-goody cunt-box."

When pressed, Sheriff Maynor said, "Jesus, kid, can't you leave it alone? What do you want me to do, fingerprint Jesus' head? You know how much money that would cost? Why don't you go to college or something and leave me the hell alone?"

Cliff Hollins, junior at Hooks High and somewhat of a nerd, said, "It wouldn't cost that much to run prints." Hollins, who mail-orders police supplies like handcuffs and night-vision lenses, as well as finger-printing kits, has said several times that he wants to join the FBI when he graduates, but most of the kids at Hooks think that he is too big of a pussy.

"He'd probably shoot his dick off," Shawn Wint said.

Tommy Green, who said he hadn't heard anything about the vandalism, even though he was seen earlier walking his dog Rosco past the area where the incident occurred, agreed.

"Yeah," Tommy said. "I think he's a fag."

"By the way," Tommy went on, without being prompted, "I was with my girlfriend, if anyone asks."

Tommy's girlfriend, Betsy Fitzgerald, however, does not corroborate Tommy's story, but told me not to say anything because Ray Carter was at her house that night, having snuck in the window after her parents had gone to sleep.

"Do you know what 'anal' means?" Betsy asked.

The gun that Beula Givens fired into the air was the same gun her husband Kenneth had used to shoot himself in the face. Most people around town think it was because his grocery store was deep in debt.

"Nobody ever paid," Beula Givens has been heard to say. "He'd let them run up a bill for cigarettes and beer, but no one would ever pay."

Alma George has a different story, however. "He killed hisself to get away from her. I'm just her neighbor and sometimes I want to kill myself."

"We're not all like that," my mother said, reading the half-written article over my shoulder. "We don't all tear up things and fire shotguns and drink too much." She poked my shoulder, hard. "You're not going to do that. You're better than that."

"Yes, ma'am," I told her.

"God, I hate fags," Tommy Green said.

Later in the day, after news of the Mayor's disparaging comment about the townspeople and their religion had mysteriously gotten out, the mayor, glaring at me as if I'd had something to do with it, had this to say:

"There's a lot of subtlety and nuance to this job that I'm still learning. I hope a stupid and insensitive comment on my part doesn't damage my chances for re-election next year."

The mayor then grabbed my tape recorder and pulled it close. "Print that, asshole," he said.

Cecil Allen, former mayor, thinks that this vandalism is a sign of something far worse.

"There are a lot of drugs in this town," the former mayor said. "And a lot of apathy. Kids dropping out of school, neighbors wanting to shoot people, policemen who sleep on the job. It's going to Hell in a handcart. If I was still running this show, things would be different."

"No one listens to that old coot," Mayor Williams responded. "Sonofabitch calls me three or four times a day. Thinks he still runs this damn town."

Still, the former mayor does have a point. Last year, out of a senior class of almost a hundred that began the school year, four kids dropped out of school, one was arrested for possession and manufacturing of crystal meth, and two out of forty-seven girls were or became pregnant during the year.

"What do you want me to do about that?" the mayor said. "Jesus H. Christ, kid."

"It's a pattern," said Principal Lassiter. "It's all over in small towns like this. You just teach the ones you can and forget about the rest of them. They'll end up in a wrench factory making six-fifty an hour and wishing they'd done something with their life, or in jail. That's harsh, but that's the way it is."

For now, police are asking people to take down their Christmas lights and decorations.

"If the lights and decorations aren't up," Sheriff John Maynor said, "the vandals won't have anything to destroy."

"That's his solution?" the former mayor said.

Responding to the sheriff's edict, Alma George said, "I'm not taking down my lights. Jesus is staying right up there until after New Years. I taped his head back on. Done a good job. You can hardly notice. I just thank God they didn't take it with them. No telling what they would have done."

Neither the sheriff nor the mayor would comment when asked what they thought the vandals would have done to Jesus' head.

Tommy Green said, "Fuck, why didn't we think of that? That old bitch might have paid to have it back."

"Whatever, man," Shawn Wint said. "I mean, it's nice that she tries, Mrs. Farris, but why doesn't she just shut the hell up and let me take the Vo-Tech courses?"

Earlier in the year, just after Thanksgiving to be exact, Tommy Green was heard saying, "I fucking hate Christmas decorations."

Speculation is that Tommy walked in on his father and their next door neighbor Kerry Parker sometime around Christmas three years ago. Kerry is a man. I know it sounds like a girl's name, but it's a man.

"You could see them glowing red in the Christmas lights across the street," Tommy said, staring off at nothing anyone else could see. "I hate him," he said, wiping at his cheek with the heel of his hand. "I c-c-can't s-stand him."

Just before the press deadline, Ralph Wint called to say that he was not going to be wearing a diaper any time soon.

"I fought in the war," Wint said. About the shotgun blast he said only, "I thought I was going to die. I thought 'I lived through D-Day and now I'm going to be shot in my underwear with diarrhea dribbling down my leg'."

"We'll still be patrolling tonight," Sheriff Maynor told me, sighing. "If they're out there, we'll get them, though I don't think they'll be out there tonight. I think they'll be hiding because they're afraid of us, and they know we'll be out there."

"I ain't afraid of shit," Tommy Green said. "I mean, not that he's talking about me."

"If I hadn't of clipped we would of won that game," Floyd Holt said, dreamy-eyed. "I still think about it. It was the playoffs. We might of won state."

"It's not that big a deal," Deputy Higgins said. "Jesus H. Christ, it was a football game twenty years ago. Who cares?"

The mayor was unavailable for final comment. His secretary, who is not bad looking, although she has never married and lives with her aging mother, said she thought he had gone to the horse track.

"He had a big wad of bills," she said. "And he was humming. He always hums when he's going to the track."

"I miss my husband," Beula Givens said, caressing her shotgun.

When asked by the sheriff's and the mayor's office if he was going to print the article, Darrell Simmons, editor of *The Bearcat*, responded, "Christ on toast, there's nothing else to print except meth lab busts. Besides, everyone knows everyone else's business here anyway. I can't see who it's going to hurt."

"In a handcart," the former mayor stated. "Mark my words."

Museum Of My Bedroom

Alexis Ivy

There's a map on the wall, *Indian Tribes*
of America, and another map of the Union
divided by the civil war. There's also a rubbing
I took of Doc Holliday's grave stone,
and three swiped Jolly Rodger flags.
I've got a copy of the last shot taken
of Jim Morrison, plus a black and white
of my dad at nineteen hung over.

In a corner stacked cigar boxes not too high,
where I keep my savings: a Motel 6 room key,
bus schedule to Joshua Tree National Park,
a chunk of could-be-Hawaiian lava, a cholla
cactus twig, and a slice of petrified wood.

On top of my bureau, jokers from eighty decks
of cards and a tin of skeleton keys I feel sorry for,
fortunes, some from Chinese cookies,
some from *Zoltar*, a lucky penny from when
the luck ran out, two bullet shells, one
from the quarry bottom, one from
when we went to Yellowstone.

On my desk are things that came before my time:
Olympia typewriter from the fifties, a bowl
of heart-shaped stones, animal teeth, ammonites.
Also a frog's leg taken out of context,
a deer antler, an entire beehive.

I keep the windowsills empty.
The floor's a scatter of sheet music hi-ho
work songs, *A Book of Convincing Legends*,
a basket of corks, the decks of cards
(minus jokers) I use to practice flicking.

I collect cigarette butts, ticket stubs,
pencil shavings, and for no good reason—
dead lighters. O, how I will save
the broken down, my heavy
load, my sole responsibility.

Turning Fifty

Judy Ireland

I take my years to bed with me,
make room beneath my best-intentioned covers,
throw my arm across
and feel the lumpy consistency
of a life's body, aging.
I gather myself in—restless limbs,
eyes that look for faces
that haven't seen light in years.

There were summers, before breasts,
when I played outdoors without a shirt.
Every third year, the lilac bush bloomed large,
and the liquid light-purple smell came in
through my bedroom window.
There were hard winters, when ice broke the surface
of everything, and frost made cruel floral patterns
on the glass outer door. There were years when
people died, and we kept putting on dresses.

This night will be too short.
        I have saved no one I intended

And the Wind

Wanda Lea Brayton

for Richard Kurtz

There is an ecstatic weaving
understood by those who stitch songs of their souls
onto dry parchment, suddenly bewildered
by the slow unfolding of evening's breath.

The warmth of autumn stirs, wanes
upon the hearth, moves us beyond reckoning.

We whisper invention,
look to undiscovered continents within ourselves,
forgetting to carry a compass, yet not requiring its guidance,
sensing the direction of true north.

His mountain lies in sweet repose, blanketed by fierce beauty,
a simple stroke of brilliance he acknowledges
each morning with glistening eyes.

Leaves fall, a gentle glissade. He gathers a stem, a stone,
a blade of burnished grass and pockets their courage.
He curls his fingers in a sigh, knowing evolution is inevitable

and the wind remains untamed.

Rope Burns

Margery Kreitman

On the first day of spring, 1958, Miss Woodcock, our fearless gym teacher, decided to test us on our rope-climbing skills. I had almost made it to the top several times before but never quite succeeded. This time I was determined. It was a "do or die" moment and my whole fifth grade career, not to mention my worth as a human being depended on it.

I wasn't exactly sure if I liked Miss Woodcock. I was fascinated but uncomfortable with her short-cropped hair and unapologetically muscular biceps and calves. Miss Woodcock hung around with my music teacher, Miss Goldman, who I adored because she was sweet and demure in her little below-the-knee shirtwaist dresses. When Miss Goldman led us in songs, her twinkling blue eyes lit up whenever we hit the right notes. I had heard that Miss Woodcock and Miss Goldman lived together in the same house and that they were two poor old spinsters, which meant they never married and that I was supposed to feel sorry for them. But I never did because, in truth, they seemed perfectly happy to me.

One by one my fellow classmates clambered a quarter or a third of the way up the rope—or failed to climb at all—and gave up. Finally it was my turn. Miss Woodcock called my name and I jumped up to the mat with lightning speed. I spit in my hands, rubbed them together, and then shimmied up the heavily braided rope as easy as a monkey up a tree. Wearing my lucky red-and-white-striped polo shirt, my favorite Lee dungarees, and my brother's old black-and-white PF Flyers, I felt completely in my element. Even the fact that I had fallen asleep the night before chewing a gooey wad of Bazooka Bubble Gum, which led the next morning to my mother having to hack out a big hunk of my hair and leaving a conspicuously large divot in the back of my head; even that certain bit of humiliation did not deter me from my goal.

I took hold of the hard yellow braid and pulled steadily and mightily hand over hand. My arms were strong and sure, and as I wrapped the rope around my feet, I effortlessly hoisted my supple little body higher and higher. Halfway up, and I had energy to spare. Three-quarters of the way, and I hadn't even broken a sweat. Clearly there was no stopping me now. I gave it two more powerful tugs, and without even realizing it, my head bumped the top of the gym. *Oh my God*, I said to myself a bit stunned, *I'm there!*

I slapped the ceiling with the palm of my hand, then twice more to make sure everyone could see, especially the boys who had always doubted me. I felt a rush of exhilaration. There I was—the top of the rope, the top of the world. I knew in that instant that I had done what no girl in my class, maybe even my whole school, had ever done before.

I was certain that this sensational coup would catapult my popularity, especially with the boys, and from then on, *I* would be the one they all desired. I had never been the prettiest or the smartest girl in my class, but I scored points with my sense of humor and athleticism. But today I was the winner, and today I most assuredly would be on the top of every boy's "list." Especially George Taft. I was crazy about George. He was strong and confident, smart and handsome, and he was the most popular boy in my class. "Dear Diary," I wrote daily.

"Please shine George Taft's ever-lovin', dreamy green eyes on me, and *please, please, please* make him mine."

By fifth grade we'd already devised a system for keeping track of who was on top and who was not. We called them "lists." Every day we jotted the names next to the numbers in the order of who we liked best. Of course, everyone wanted to be everyone else's *Number One.* And every day in class we secretly passed our lists back and forth, unfolding and reading them as we crouched inside our little wooden desks.

I savored my moment at the top of the rope, relishing the attention of every eye upon me, every face in awe, as my tiny classmates gazed up from their rows, sitting cross-legged on the shiny, waxed gymnasium floor. I spotted the bouncy red ponytail of Buffy Sloan, whose mother was my Brownie leader and who, except for the time I dropped and dragged the American flag through the mud in the Memorial Day parade, referred to me as *promising material* for the Mariners. In the second row sat my friend and fellow goofball Jimmy Markowitz, who had a crush on me, and made me laugh till I rolled on the floor in hysterical fits with his incomparable impersonations of Soupy Sales. In the back, off by herself, was Audrey Morton, who secretly ate chalk in the cloakroom and in whom I took solace that no matter how unpopular I might ever feel, there was always someone who would never make it on anyone's "list." And then there was Patty Layton, who the year before had sung the winning song, "Que Sera, Sera" in the talent show, and took home first prize. It was two weeks ago today in the very same gymnasium that Buffy Sloan, Patty Layton, and I sang in this year's Valentine's Day talent show. We called ourselves "The Three Freckles," aptly named because we all three were splattered with brown specks from head to toe. We rehearsed every day and we were good. We could even harmonize. We sang the hit song, "The Book of Love." My solo line was "Chapter two you tell her, you're never, never, never, never never ever gonna part," which I delivered kneeling, Four Tops style, and the audience went wild.

I had big plans for "The Three Freckles." I wanted to get us on Ted Mack's *Amateur Hour.* I had watched it on TV enough to know that we were as good if not better than some of the acts, like The Munchausers, a family of yodelers from Minnesota, or this fat kid from Iowa with his hair greased down with Brylcreem, who played "America the Beautiful" on a blade of grass. But in the eleventh hour, Buffy dropped out, choosing baton-twirling lessons over our rehearsals, and it wasn't the same anymore with just two freckles, so we broke up.

After our spectacular performance that day, I found tiny pink candy hearts on my desk, "Be Mine," etched in little lavender letters. I was sure it was from George. I waited all day for him to approach me. But he never did. After school that day, Buffy said she forgot to tell me she saw Jimmy Markowitz leave little candy hearts on my desk during recess.

Still holding tight atop the rope, I noticed Jimmy Markowitz waving up at me, wildly throwing kisses. I didn't respond. I did not have time. I was on a mission to find George. I searched every row and every face, amazed I hadn't spotted him. I couldn't imagine where he was. Had he left early today? Gone to the bathroom? Had band practice? I searched for his red flannel shirt. Finally, I caught sight of him huddled down in the second row. I tried to catch his eye; signal, wave, cough, all but shout his name. He seemed preoccupied. He turned his head ever so slightly, and for a moment I saw his face. *Here I am, George*, I silently screamed, *I'm up here. Look! Look at me!* But his face was not gazing up adoringly; rather it was angled toward the back row, smiling adoringly and utterly entranced by the charms of Jill Cabernet.

Jill Cabernet, with the dazzling curly blond hair and kick-pleat skirt, was the prettiest and most popular girl in school. She would never rope climb or, for that matter, gallop around the schoolyard whinnying like a horse, which I did every recess. Jill was a real girl; the quintessential peaches and cream to my rough elbows, freckles, and buckteeth. And she had the cutest dimples and most adorable giggle to go with them. Jill and I had rarely spoken, and most times I don't think I even existed in her world. But there was one time at recess, I could swear I caught her watching me out of the corner of my eye as I hurdled over the seesaw in one gigantic leap.

While I vainly struggled to attract George Taft's attention, my hands grew sweaty on the rope, and before I knew it, I felt myself slipping. I looked down at Miss Woodcock. She appeared forlorn, shaking her head as if to say *This poor girl is done for.* "I can do it," I insisted, claiming a momentary lapse. After all, I had always been the best girl in every sport, often as good or better than some of the boys. That was a good thing until junior high when the same boys who admired my grade school prowess shunned me, even when I wore a dress.

"You had better get down from there, young lady. Rope climbing is not for the faint of heart," Miss Woodcock proclaimed, addressing the children who were looking up at me agape. She was obviously taking this opportunity to illustrate to her young charges the dire consequences of making such a foolhardy mistake, of showing off: to teach them a valuable life lesson. "I've said it before and I'll say it again. Rope climbing is dangerous. Girls beware!" Her words reverberated in my head. The room began to spin. My arms felt rubbery and weak. Then, I lost my grip.

I dropped like a plane in sudden heavy turbulence, my hands burning on the twisted, hard cord, ripping the armpits of my lucky red-and-white polo as I descended out of control. I clenched my legs tight around the rope in a desperate attempt to somehow brake the runaway train, the friction rubbing hot through my blue dungarees, scorching the insides of my tender thighs. The big rope swung and twisted, and I clutched it with all I had left in me, and somehow by the grace of God I managed to catch myself a quarter of the way down. Hanging on for dear life, I hung suspended in midair, silently swinging like a giant pendulum. I felt far away and alone. It was just me up there, and I longed to feel my feet on the big knot at the bottom of the rope. I don't know if it was Miss Woodcock's damning words or the sound of Jill Cabernet's tantalizing giggle that pushed me over the edge, but in that moment, I was certain that this was not where I belonged.

So, I let go. Accompanied by my classmates' horrified gasps, I plummeted, hitting the worn gray mat with a quiet, desperate thud. A bit dazed, I looked up and saw Miss Woodcock hunched over me. I noticed for the first time she was covered with freckles, and her front two teeth protruded, same as mine. "Are you all right?" she asked with a ponderous frown. My mouth quivered and my chest heaved as I glanced around the room. The children were all quiet and staring. *Where is George? Surely he will come to my rescue.* I spotted him in the back row, his figure somewhat blurry through my falling tears. All I could make out was that his hands were clasped over his mouth, and his body was trembling. *Oh, my gosh.* I thought. *Is he so upset, so shaken up by my near catastrophe?* But on second glance, he was not upset at all. In fact, he was trying his darnedest to stifle a guffaw.

Miss Woodcock helped me to my feet and asked for a volunteer to take me to the nurse. After a long silence, Jill Cabernet raised her hand. I begrudgingly accepted her help. Limping down the hall-way, her arm supporting mine, I stole a glance at her face. Her cheeks seemed particularly rosy and flushed: her skin, warm, soft, almost moist. But our eyes never met, and we did not speak. She dropped me at the nurse's office.

"I can't believe you did that," she whispered low. Ashamed, I turned away, determined she would not see my final defeat. *How mean she is*, I sulked. *Is that why she offered to take me to the nurse? To rub it in?* But then I felt her hand softly touch my bare arm. It rested there for what seemed like minutes. She glanced into my eyes, and I found myself looking back.

"You were amazing," she said softly and smiled.

Before I could speak, she rushed off. I stood staring in disbelief as she rounded the corner, and then she was gone.

Later, back in class, I was bruised but not really hurt. When the bell rang at three o'clock, I lingered for a while at my desk, eating the candy hearts I had saved from Valentine's Day. I took out my list and erased George Taft from number one. In its place, I wrote a new name, "Jill Cabernet." Then I folded the list neatly and put it back inside my desk.

To Be A Cowboy

William Jolliff

I knew a man—should I call him a *boy*?—
who grew younger. It was a conscious choice,
a decision. He'd grown weary with numbers,
the lucrative flashes of the green screen.

But this is the magical part, the movie:
He hitched to Idaho and learned to cowboy.
Big hat, bowed legs, hard work on a desert ranch,
skidding slopes that would spook a mule.

That's when he began to believe in heaven.
Having turned twenty at forty, who wouldn't?
He'd fled to the open range like a Monarch
finds its home in Mexico. But then he left it.

Maybe heaven is an easier place to get to
than to stay. That's not to say you shouldn't go,
or that heaven's not a good place to have been—
only that driving needs don't stop driving.

My Cousin Matthew

Hannah Selinger

Matthew was six-years-old that afternoon when the
slow mechanical drawl of an aging
yellow school bus opened two doors to sprawling
pavement. The predictable march down steps
ended unpredictably. First, a young hand reaching outward
to stop the curious momentum of a younger brother. Then:
a speeding corvette, slick licorice in the midday sun.
No child's hand could have restricted fate
and when the car made contact and Matthew flew—*learned to fly*—
history condensed. Fifteen years later, we buried him, an
atrophied twenty-one. What was left of that small life he spent asleep.
Maybe there was beauty in the last
moments of childhood clarity: a lacquered bus,
the stripe of sun across the ground, grass clippings,
reminders of spring, rebirth, changing seasons.
Or, the gliding motion of that car, soaring through space,
finite majesty of the ebony beast that would extinguish life.

Still Life With Lou Gehrig

I follow you up flights of stairs,
worried you'll fall, consumed
knowing that each step presents a new danger.
You taught me to walk and to swim.
Was it that long ago that you carried me,
unburdened, up flights like these?

In six months, the sinewy
muscles of your legs have dwindled,
now rubber bands capable of collapse.
The house is one of infirm, all the
accoutrement of illness to remind us:
How life has changed!

Remember when I could not keep up?
Remember the mornings when you left
before we woke, cresting hills with the dog's
leash in hand? You were an athlete,
scoffing at our physical weaknesses. How lazy,
your little girls, who preferred TV to nature.

I thought I had more time.

Though 29, I wanted a daddy for longer.

Life's passage seems too short, or

wrought with anguish we did not predict.

It is not fair, we say. And yet,

we know that nothing is, not your

rubber band legs or stooped, slow gait.

This is the setting sun and we watch your

colors fade from pink to orange into

dark. I am still behind and will not let you

fall, but who will be at the end, at the

banister to break my own probable

stumble?

Misdemeanors

Karin Lin-Greenberg

You want to know where the street signs are? I've got them. I've got Princeton Lane and Harvard Corner and Yale Drive. I've got Dartmouth Avenue and Cornell Street, too. I've got all the Ivies, stashed in the back of my closet. Each night after I got a rejection letter from a college, I went out and stole the street sign that matched the school rejecting me. It was easy; I didn't even need any tools to turn the loose screws they used to affix the signs to the metal poles.

It started on a Monday with Harvard and their "We regret to inform you...," and it ended the next Thursday with Columbia and "The pool of applicants was large and qualified." Screw them all. And screw Mrs. Sandler, the guidance counselor who made me join all those extracurriculars—band and fencing and art club and reading to the blind and Key Club and Academic Quiz Bowl and Spanish Cinemaphiles, even though I neither speak Spanish nor am a cinemaphile. I became overextended, which led to my B+ average, which led to my lack of admittance into the Ivy League, which led to my not having anywhere to go next year. "You'll take a gap year," said Mrs. Sandler once the last rejection flowed in. I sat in her office in the blue fuzzy chair that smelled like Fritos, stared across the desk at Mrs. Sandler, and fought the urge to push over her mug of coffee onto her computer's keyboard.

Things are not going any better at home than they are at school. My mother is the president of the Residents' Association of Windmill

Village, and she makes me go along with her to all the meetings so I can take the minutes. When she was first elected, I agreed to do this because I thought it would pad my college applications. Wrong.

Tonight's meeting is focused on the missing street signs. The residents have worked themselves into a panic, convinced themselves that some thugs have invaded the tranquility of Windmill Village and the missing signs are just the tip of the iceberg. Soon, they are sure, mailboxes will be knocked over, and then windows will be smashed, and then their expensive cars will be keyed. "All hell will break loose," says Dr. Woods. I think the residents of Windmill Village are secretly excited about possible chaos; they are protected by the best insurance policies, and some minor criminal action would stir up their monotonous lives.

"Who knows who'll be the next victim?" says Mrs. Detmer, who lives on Whippoorwill Lane. Trust me, I want to tell her that the people who live on the bird streets will be just fine. I have no interest in Blue Jay Drive, Robin Avenue, or Sparrow Street. My theft was confined only to the signs in Ivy Court.

"Now, now," says my mother, "we shouldn't be too alarmed. I've talked to Joe about using sturdier bolts for the replacement signs." My mother is wearing a goddamned navy blue suit and stockings and high heels for this meeting because it is the most important part of her month. Right now I hate her, and I hate her Styrofoam cup of coffee that is stained around the top with the lipstick she put on especially for this meeting. I might hate all adults and their lack of ability to give good advice, and their general stupidity, and their small, boring worlds. Maybe I *will* take a gap year and travel to Peru or Thailand, or maybe I'll climb Mt. Kilimanjaro and bring my street signs, all eight of them, and plant them on top.

"There are hoodlums on the loose," says Mr. Rutkowski, and I snort at the word "hoodlums" and then pretend the snort was a cough when a handful of residents look over at me. I'm only supposed to sit in the back of the room and take notes quietly. But I'm tired of doing what I'm supposed to be doing because where has that gotten me? A one-way ticket to another year in Windmill Village, raking leaves in the fall, helping my mother make sure no one has unapproved Christmas lights hanging in December, a minimum wage lifeguard job in the summer. I can't stand it, any of it, and I slide out the door into the cool night. No one notices when I get up to leave, taking my notepad and my minutes full of scrawled notes about hoodlums and hooligans and shenanigans.

I head to Avian Court, stretching my arms as I walk, as if I'm preparing to compete in the breaststroke. It's lucky I'm tall and the tops of the signposts aren't beyond my reach. I get to Whippoorwill Lane and reach up and twist the bolt connecting the green metal sign to the pole, and the sign slips off with a clank, and I shove the sign down the back of my pants and pull my sweater down over it. The lights of a car shine around the corner and then I see Mrs. Fulton in her Volvo, and she waves and I lift my hand and wave back and smile, and I'm sure I look exactly like a nice kid with a bright future just out for an innocent evening stroll.

Luck Isn't Clever

Daneen Bergland

Luck merely drives the truck
on the right side of the road
while you play with the radio
because it knows how to follow
rules and anyway it likes
the way you look from that angle
with your hair lit up like that,
the dashboard on one side,
the other, a fleet of stars.

Luck's beauty is ridiculous,
like a sixteenyearold farm girl's.

Danger is luck's sexy cousin.

Luck makes it hard sometimes
to be really happy.

In a gust of wind Luck
watches your skirt bell up
around your thighs and smiles.
Luck likes the underwear you've chosen.

On Facebook and Loss

On Facebook a dead woman's tragedy unfolds like a grease-stained map. There are unloved messages, not to mention old lovers flirting with their spouses. There are so many ways to be burned. So I ask my friend how's your dad? He's dead is the first line of our hackneyed exchange. And I wish there were a different answer than thank you for sorry. You see, I've not suffered permanence yet. So time is impossible to measure. So I slide my hand over the opened fold like the paper needs comforting and give her a perfectly parallel sentence I hope is more salve than a note sung in unison by a choir on a screen. I've noticed how some people can pick up a pen like a child plays with a stick as if the stick already knew what it wanted to be without the child telling it. But how I feel belongs to the people I love. So I wait for them all to die off, I guess. This feels sort of like a game and my hand's on the spinner. In the meantime the greatest loss I've suffered up until now was cigarettes. Yet this vague face of the dead man my age keeps coming up as a suggestion. I once spent a whole day keeping his secret. And when we were children he stuck his tongue with me to the frozen bars just to feel the effects. Until we sat bleeding, our mouths stuffed with paper.

They Will Never Know It Was Me

So lucky am I to be born on the day
a man got stung by so many bees
they filled his mouth till he had to chew and swallow them.
They stung his eyes till he could no longer hear
anything but the hum of God.
He jumped in the river and they drowned his dog.
A year later he fell, and when his ear hit the ground,
a bee popped out.
He could hear again the buzz
of his pretty wife whispering
how I love you darling, head to tail, whales to bees.
The news says a woman stings herself once a day to cure her blindness.
The news says every third bite you take has a bumblebee in it.
The news says each day we are a thousand fewer bees
closer to the end of the world.
But I just saw a honeybee French kiss a primrose.
And boy I was glad to get some good news for a change.
I feel sorry for people who slash the air with their hands,
who consider them the garden's finks and so fear the lilies.
If I caught one now I would pet its velvet very carefully.

I would hold it up to my ear and listen
to its little heart beat: okay okay okay okay
before sending it in an envelope marked simply "from January"
to the castle of the president to wish him luck.

I Should Have Been Dead

Either way: floating belly up, naked, alone
in the ammonium nitrate
methyl bromide river at night.

Or belly down in the winter,
when my head slammed
the thin glaze of ice

and I peered through the web
I'd made in its black glass,
with the river's breath

trapped behind it.
All the leeches, ticks,
and child molesters.

All the rusty lids
pried off cans of toxic waste
shat out of the ravine.

I scooped the insides out
like pumpkins and smeared them
on my jeans. How I dared

electric fences to catch me wet
with a fistful of smashed pennies
while I played by the trains.

When I longed for twisters
that shrank in the distance
because I wasn't ever quite frightened

enough. Swimming the abandoned ink
of rock quarries. And later, when my white Buick
took flight, caught the lip of a ditch

in a whiteout. Or earlier, my first blackout
and the necklace it left,
seventeen anonymous love bites.

And again and again, I overflowed ashtrays,
shrines to sleepless nights, to the phone calls
from women tattooed with fist prints

with the windows locked tight
blowing smoke into the cradle
and the bricks still seething.

For the men who said I could be the one,
if only, and sent a chain of rug burns
up my bony spine.

For the dead pilot light.
For the wave of flame, and the pink blossom
of skin seared suddenly awake.

Class Notes

Lawrence F. Farrar

What inspired Everett Finch to submit an item to the "1970 Class Notes" remains a mystery to him to this day. In any case, one spring afternoon in 1995 he settled himself at his computer and composed an entry for *Alumni Jottings*, his Fremont College alumni magazine. In that submission he informed classmates—sort of—about his activities over the preceding twenty-five years.

His comments were brief:

Greetings to all you 70ers. From what I read in this column, everybody seems to be a doctor, a lawyer, or Ph.D. physicist some-where. Way to go. As some might remember, after we departed the old quad, I managed to get drafted and shipped off to Vietnam. Wasn't there long though, as things were coming apart. No war stories to report. Came back and entered my father's clothing business (Finch's Menswear) and later on became the president. We have three stores in Southern California. I'm still married to Sheryl, and we have one son, Kyle, who is trying to be a musician in New York. Been in the same house in La Jolla for the last twenty years. We keep busy with golf and travel (last year we made a river cruise in France). We haven't had much contact with classmates over the years, so if any of you find your way to sunny California, we'd love to have you stop by.
Ev Finch

It had been a selective truth telling. Finch had, for example, omitted the facts that he'd been discharged from the army for *lack of aptitude*; that, deeming Finch incompetent, his father had clung to the company reins until the very day of his death two years before; that Sheryl was involved in a long-standing liaison with a golf pro ten years her junior; and that Kyle had bounced in and out of drug rehab programs since he was fifteen.

Finch was a slight man, with languid bluish eyes and sallow skin absolutely unaffected by San Diego's eternal sunshine. He was given to wearing chinos, button-down Oxford shirts, and buckskin shoes. A vulnerable person, by no measure could Finch be described as a hard charger. He would like to have been one—indeed yearned to be one—but he wasn't. No matter how deeply you might have probed into his nature, you would have chanced upon no hidden reservoir of assertiveness. He smiled and nodded, or sometimes just nodded, and pretty much went along with whatever others suggested, a foible people—notably his wife—happily exploited.

When he was alive, Everett's father had declared that, when they handed out gumption, his son never reached the head of the line. Finch yearned to prove him wrong, to demonstrate he had the moral fiber to stand up for himself. But, his inability to cope with his wife's affair, his son's run-ins with the law, or even the destruction of his flower beds by the neighbor's Spaniel lent credence to the claim. He could just as well have written in his "Class Notes" submission, *My life has been one of invincible mediocrity.*

The flame of ambition had never burned brightly; it had made no purchase on his soul. Truth be told, rather than concerning himself with his clothing business, management of which he ceded to Paul Medwick, a former clerk in the San Diego store, Finch preferred to putter in his garden. This despite the fact his roses burned and his orchids drooped. Typically, after sending off his electronic missive to *Alumni Jottings*, Finch had strolled out to inspect his less demanding herbs. Rosemary, sage, and basil all appeared to be prospering. Perhaps, he thought, he ought to have mentioned his green thumb in his "Class Notes" submission.

When the alumni magazine rattled through his mail slot, Finch immediately scrutinized his own entry. He rarely saw his name in print and liked the feeling it produced. Establishing him as a class member in good standing among his successful peers, the piece gave his life definition, realized a vision of himself as he hoped to be.

Nonetheless, he doubted many classmates remembered him, and he considered it unlikely anyone would respond to the suggestion they "stop by." He dropped the magazine on a coffee table and forgot about it. Forgot about it, that is, until a Saturday afternoon two weeks later when a jangling telephone intruded on his contemplation of the surf teasing the beach below his house.

"Is this Everett Finch, Class of 1970?" The male caller's tone was familiar, even if his voice was not. "Nick Devlin here."

Nick Devlin? Finch's mind ferreted through his memory bank—but found no deposit.

"I'm afraid, I don't recall..."

"Come on, Ev. You must remember me. Lived right down the hall from you sophomore year. You forgot all those beer pong games?"

Finch recalled no beer pong games, and the man's name simply didn't register.

"You say we were in the same dorm?"

"Right. Plus we had two or three classes together, late night bull sessions, some great fraternity parties. Anyway, I spotted your invitation in the "1970 Class Notes." Passing through and thought it would be a kick to stop by and chat about the old days."

Stop by? It had been a throwaway line; now, as if struck full force by a coastal landslide, Finch experienced the crushing weight of obligation. "Well, perhaps if you would like to come by..."

"Sounds great. How about this afternoon? I'm at a hotel right here in La Jolla. Got a rental car. Sure I can find you."

"This afternoon?" Nonplussed, but unable to conjure up a plausible reason why the man should not come by, Finch said, "Okay. Perhaps in an hour or so?"

"Terrific, Ev. I'm practically on my way."

Finch fidgeted by the phone. Unease enveloped him like the smog that drifted down the coast and scarped the hills above his house.

When Finch unlatched the front door, an involuntary bolt of distaste raced through him. A thickset man peered in at him from behind aviator-style dark glasses. Caught in the sunlight, the man's sparse hair, whatever its original hue, shone absolutely black, as did his pathetically thin mustache. His outfit—rust-colored trousers supported by a white belt, polished white shoes, a blue polyester shirt, and an ill-fitting gray sport coat—offended Finch's haberdasher's eye, as did the gold neck chain that finished off the ensemble. Devlin looked like he'd twirled right off a 70s disco floor.

"Long time, no see," Devlin said, extending his hand. "How goes it, Ev?"

"Fine. Nice to see you," Finch replied, conscious as they shook hands of the jeweled rings glittering on the man's pinkies.

"Well, no point standing here gabbing on the step," Devlin said. "Aren't you going to invite me in?"

"I thought we might go out on the verandah—I guess most people call it a deck nowadays. We have a nice view of the Pacific," Finch said.

He guided his visitor through the living room. Devlin paused and raised his glasses; his deep brown eyes roved across the polished wooden floor, the mission style furniture, heavy and dark, and the California-themed paintings and prints (clipper ships off Point Loma, mission padres saving the heathen, and desert landscapes) that festooned the walls. Passing through a sliding door, they stepped out onto the deck where Finch gestured to one of the canvas-covered chairs at a glass-topped table.

"Please. Have a seat...Mr. Devlin."

"Come on Ev. No need for all the formality. It's Nick. Just good old Nick."

"Were you really in my class? I don't seem to remember..." Finch showed an expression of puzzled geniality.

"Yep. I was a transfer. Came after freshman year." Devlin again lifted his glasses and gazed at the ocean. "You're right. Great view. I bet it costs a mint for a house on the water like this."

In fact, tour guides often pointed the house out as representative of Southern California's Spanish colonial architecture. Sited behind low walls and surrounded by a palm-studded garden, the Finch home displayed a white stucco exterior, a red tile roof, and arched windows.

"My family's had this place for years and years, but I gather it *is* rather expensive to buy a home in this area now."

"Rather expensive? There's the understatement of the year. Ev, old buddy, you're living on the Gold Coast."

Finch considered his shoes. "Perhaps you would like a drink."

"I was wondering *when* you'd ask. Scotch on the rocks would suit me just fine."

Finch went into the house and fetched a bottle of Chivas Regal, two glasses, and a bucket of ice. Carrying these items on a tray, he rejoined his guest, who was now leaning on the deck's rail observing surfers dancing in on curling waves.

"Great," Devlin said. "I see you brought the bottle."

Finch poured them each a glass. His visitor obviously wanted it; and Finch, already feeling pangs of inviter's remorse—if there was such a thing—needed it.

"Welcome," Finch said and raised his glass.

"To the good old days," Devlin replied and downed his drink in two convulsive gulps.

Finch hesitated. "Yes. To the good old days." Whatever they might have been.

"Say, Ev, you wouldn't have any snacks would you? Nuts or something. I missed lunch and..."

"Oh. My apologies. I should have brought something with the drinks. Usually my wife looks after these things. How about some chips? I think we have a nice avocado dip."

"Speaking of the Mrs.—am I going to have a chance to say hello?"

"She had a golf lesson this afternoon. Expect her home any time."

Finch went into the house to gather some snack items. Who was this person? He *did* seem vaguely familiar—or did he?

By the time Finch returned with the chips and dip, Devlin had fortified himself with another drink. "Great Scotch. Nothing but the best for you folks in La Jolla, I guess."

"Well, I expect it's a rather ordinary brand and..."

A freshening breeze set the table umbrella to rustling and flapping above their heads. Keening gulls cavorted and hung over the water. An odor redolent of salt water and seaweed rose up and engulfed the deck and its occupants.

"Always smell like this?" Finch said, making a face as if he'd lifted the cover of a garbage can and taken a whiff.

"Just the ocean," Finch said. "I guess you notice it more when there's an onshore breeze.

"Hey, Ev, speaking of smells, you remember the time somebody pissed on the Dean's morning newspaper and his cat? They never found out who did it."

Finch stared at him blankly. The story had no resonance, triggered no recollection of wet paper or damp cat.

Undeterred, Devlin pushed on. "Got a confession to make. It was me. Guess I was pretty snockered that night." Cackling at the recollection, Devlin freshened his Scotch. "Want some?" he said.

Finch shook his head. Who *was* this person? And why had he brought him into his home?

"Well, what have you been up to all these years?" Devlin said. "Looks like you did all right for yourself. Yes, sir. All right."

"I guess I pretty much said it all in the 'Class Notes'." It occurred to Finch that anything more was really none of this man's business.

"Aw come on. I bet there were some hairy times over there in 'Nam."

"Not really. I was a clerk in Saigon."

"I thought you vets all had stories. Anyway, how about your business? I expect you've been a real entrepreneur." He paused. "You know, Ev, these chips are pretty stale. You probably want to get rid of them."

"Oh, I'm sorry," Finch said. Why should he be sorry? Devlin was wearing on him. Finch resolved to send Devlin on his way. He would firmly respond to this man's repellent behavior.

"Maybe you've got something else in the larder," Devlin said.

Finch studied the man's face. Removal of the sunglasses had not reassured him. Devlin's eyes, Finch thought, belonged to the sort of person who'd help himself to coins from a church poor box. Although Finch could recall no earlier association, that shifty mien struck a vaguely responsive chord. Perhaps it was simply the power of suggestion; Devlin's repeated assertion they'd been classmates.

"What about yourself? How has life treated you since our campus days?" Finch sought to probe a bit.

"Well, I wasn't as favored as some of you folks." He brushed his thumb and index fingers together, the near-universal signal for money. "Had to make it on my own—if you know what I mean. Spent a little time in the Air Force; couldn't stomach the brass and all that 'yes, sir' 'no, sir' baloney. Since then, you might say I've been a jack-of-all-trades, mostly in the entertainment industry—Atlantic City and Las Vegas." Finch decided Devlin looked like someone who cheated at cards.

"I see," Finch said. "Have you a family?" He was running out of things to say. He had to tell Devlin it was time to go. He'd surely fulfilled any required courtesy imposed on him.

"Nah. Tied the knot three times, but sent them all packing. Footloose and fancy free, that's me."

There were certainly times Finch wished *he* was footloose and fancy free. In that sense, Devlin intrigued him. Yet, a thickening scrim of apprehension wrapped about him like a shroud.

"I hoped I might get a chance to meet the little lady. She's bound to be a real looker."

Finch visualized the crow's feet, sagging underarms, ungirdled paunch, and bleached hair. "I suppose you could say that," he said.

"I'll bet you've know a few women in your day—plenty of dough, living out here on the coast." Devlin regarded his glass like a medium summoning up images from the past. "You were a real ladies' man as I recall. They always go for guys like you. I guess the scent of money comes right out of your skin."

A ladies' man? My goodness. How did Devlin come up with that curious notion?

"I expect you belong to a country club. Am I right?"

"Well, yes, but..."

"I thought so. You on the board of directors or anything?"

"Oh, no. My grandfather was a founding member. I just play golf there."

"Maybe we could play a round. You could arrange for some clubs, right?" Finch lolled back in his chair.

Manipulating the interlaced fingers on his lap, Finch hesitated. "I really don't play much anymore and..." Finch shuddered at the prospect of having to introduce this man to someone in the pro shop.

"Hey. I get it. Say no more. I'll take a rain check." Devlin's expression was one of hurt bravely borne.

"Yes. Perhaps another time."

Devlin was again filling his glass. "They doing any hiring? You know—like maybe a greeter or starter, something like that."

"Are you looking for a job?"

"Well, it wouldn't have to be at your club. Maybe you know somebody at one of the hotels or..."

"Is that why you..." As determined as he was to avoid being manipulated, nonetheless, Finch felt he was being led along like a poodle in a show ring.

"Everett. I'm home." Sheryl Finch called from inside the house. "Whose car is that in the drive?" She sounded more accusatory than inquisitive. A moment later, she came out to where the men were seated.

"Sheryl, this is Nick Devlin. He says we went to college together," Finch reported.

"Hi, Sheryl. Ev's a real joker. I didn't just *say* so; it's a fact. Of course we were in school together. Anyway, nice to meet you. Any wife of Ev Finch is a friend of mine. Get it? Any wife of..."

"I think Nick was just going to leave, so..." Finch said.

"No way. I've got plenty of time. Don't get a chance to connect like this very often." He rested his hand on Finch's shoulder. "Old pals, right?"

Finch edged away, and Sheryl looked perplexed, but camouflaged her reaction with a welcoming smile. Surveying the table, she said, "Would you like some cheese and crackers or perhaps some cashews or..."

"That would be great," Devlin said. "All Ev came up with are these chips and this green dip—whatever it is." Quality reservations notwithstanding, he had pillaged the entire tray.

Once Sheryl reentered the house, Finch said, "I'm really afraid I can't help you find a position. I don't even belong to the Rotary anymore and..."

"Gotcha. But you know what they say. Networking's the coming thing."

"Networking?"

"Yeah. Talking to people you know—or somebody they know—people who might lead you to a good situation."

"I see." Finch concocted an image of a network, focusing on the word *net*, something in which he might become entangled.

Sheryl reappeared, still sporting her golf togs. Devlin eyed her up and down and then said, "Looks like you two must have been married for a long time. Ev's just been telling me what a great wife he has."

"He has?" A look of astonishment seized control of her face. Astonishment not just that her husband might say such a thing, but that he had offered an opinion at all.

Devlin happily crunched through a handful of crackers, mounding them with Brie and chasing them down with slugs of Scotch. "Damn. That hits the spot," he said. Then, in near-seamless transition, he said, "Where's the facilities? Need to make a pit stop."

"Right through the living room; there's a guest bathroom just off the foyer."

Sauntering past Sheryl, Devlin winked and said, "I *told* Ev his wife must be a looker." Then he disappeared into the house.

"Who is he? Why is he here?" Sheryl asked. She took short, quick puffs on a cigarette.

"I told you. He said we were in college together. And, I...well, I guess in a way, I invited him."

"What does that mean?"

"I ended my 'Class Notes' entry with a kind of invitation for people to stop by, but I didn't think..." It had been, Finch concluded, a regrettable benefaction.

"Well, he's uncouth, to say the least. Show a little spunk. Send him away."

"I'm trying. I really am."

"Try harder. I'm running some errands." She ground out the cigarette under her heel on a patio stone. "He'd better be gone when I get back." Moments later the front door slammed.

"Where's the little lady" Devlin said when he reappeared after an extended absence.

"Oh, she had some errands to run. Said it was nice to meet you."

"I doubt that. Hate to tell you this, Ev, but I can't say she came across too well. How did you end up with her anyway?"

Finch nervously cleared his throat. "Come now. That is an inappropriate thing to say." There *had* to be a limit to how much of this he could tolerate.

"Hey, Ev, I call them as I see them." Devlin delivered a smirky smile.

Finch absorbed this in silence. Neither man spoke. Time dragged, as if governed by an hour glass stocked with moist sand.

"I'm really surprised you claim not to remember me," Devlin said at last. "Did you forget all about those guys in the fraternity who were ready to blackball you? Thought you were, how can I put it, not really up to their standards."

"What are you talking about?"

"Never mind that I'm the one who spoke up for you. Told them they had you all wrong. Seems to me you could be a little more appreciative."

"But, I was never in a..."

"And there was the time that professor thought we stole the answers to the chemistry exam. I suppose you don't remember that either."

"I only took biology and astronomy," Finch declared. Devlin must be mad.

"Specifics don't matter. I saved your bacon more than once. Seems to me a little bit of gratitude is in order."

"I want you to go now, Finch said as firmly as he could. "You've been extraordinarily unpleasant."

"Now, now, Ev, old boy, don't get all riled up." Refilling his glass, Devlin said, "You wouldn't have any more of this cheese would you?" The man seemed as impervious to civilized behavior as an armadillo in its shell. Had Devlin no idea of the meaning of conscience?

"You are obviously confused. We were never at school together. You must go or…"

"Or what?"

"Or I'll be forced to call…the police."

"Really? Ev, you're the one who's confused. You owe me plenty. You've just pushed it all out of your mind. It's really pretty funny." He chuckled in a derisive way.

Finch believed he was about to come undone. "Get out. Get out of my house!"

"Now what sort of attitude is that to have towards a fellow alum?"

Finch wanted to stand up to this bully; he had always wanted to stand up to those who exploited him. He had mustered all the resolve he could. Alas, it was no use pretending; it had proved inadequate. Nothing left, Finch felt himself crumbling. "What do you want?" he said in desperation. "What do you *want*?" Could Devlin be planning something rash?

"Why, I thought you'd never ask." Devlin folded his arms and gave Finch a knowing look. "Since you can't come up with a job, how about a loan?"

"A loan?"

"Yeah. A loan. Moola, lucre, money. M-O-N-E-Y. You know— for old times' sake. You've got plenty."

There had been no threats, no physical pressure; yet, Finch felt precisely as if he was being assaulted and robbed. Nothing mattered now except by some means, any means, to be rid of this obnoxious person. This intense desire crushed to nothingness his earlier inclination to assert himself, to challenge Devlin's aggression.

"Yes." Finch nodded. "Yes. That's it. Money. I'll give you money."

"No checks, just cash." Devlin brushed a clinging chunk of Brie from his chin.

Finch fanned open his billfold and extracted three one hundred dollar bills and some twenties.

"Here. It's yours. Just go... Please. Just go."

"Took you long enough." Devlin plucked the bills singly from Finch's hand, as if plucking flowers from the garden, then stuffed them into an inner pocket. "Well. Thanks for the invite and the snacks. And thanks for the loan," he said. "Good seeing you again, Ev."

Finch stared at him in dumfounded amazement, and then trailed him through the house and to the front door. Devlin trotted down the steps and hopped into a brilliantly red sports car. "Guess I'll be on my way. Regards to the little woman." Devlin waved, whipped around the circular drive, and vanished.

Relieved but still shaken, Finch sank into a deck chair and gazed at lingering smudges of light as the sun sank over the Pacific. Was Devlin that fellow expelled the second week of school for theft? No, that person's name was...what was his name? It was all so long ago and the memories were so uncertain. As perplexed as when he first picked up the phone that afternoon, Finch struggled to decipher what had happened, how it had happened, how it *could* have happened.

Sheryl discovered the missing credit cards as soon as she came home, the disappeared jewelry an hour or two later. As for the sterling silver butter knives and teaspoons, Finch surmised they'd been easier to slip into a pocket because of their size. When Sheryl denounced him, Finch nodded—nothing more.

The following month the 1970 class secretary, Annie Covington, appended a comment at the end of the "Class Notes." Finch cringed when he read:

We were certainly delighted to hear from Everett Finch after so many years. All you 70ers be sure and give him a call if you're headed San Diego way.

Your faithful servant,

A.C.

But none of them did, unless you count Nick Devlin, of whom no trace and for whom no record was ever found.

The Orchards of Cleveland

Iris Miller

I glimpsed the crows from the window
of a train on the outskirts
of Cleveland—perched on bare branches,
among the last of the apples, like birds
in a Japanese print.

In Japan I saw—not apples,
but persimmons. They hung from trees
like tiny orange suns. I ate one,
sliced, in a Tokyo izakaya
bought their image painted on a fan.
When I returned to Cleveland
I searched till I found a persimmon,
opened it up to the star at its heart,
laid its flesh on my tongue.

Actually, I have never been
to Cleveland. Also, I have never
seen a flock of crows in an apple tree.
Perhaps the trees are too small

to attract such large birds. I could change
the crows to starlings, but I love
crows the way I love persimmons.

Before I became enamored
of persimmons, I went to the top of Tokyo's
tallest building. Gazing out at miles
of glass and steel, I thought of the time
I took my two little girls down 5th Avenue
to the Empire State Building
in a blizzard, to show them New York
from a bird's eye view. We could barely
see out the window of the bus.
Yet the sign surprised me—*Visibility
zero. Observation deck closed.*
This story is true.

This also is true—after a while
my desire for persimmons faded.
I seldom thought to buy them anymore.

The crows flew away, leaving apples
behind. The train kept on moving
toward Cleveland.

How It Is

Even bedrock will not
hold, one ledge
slips, another slides.
Cars fall into ravines, cows
go wild. Now
the cows are in my head,
behind my eyes. Black
and white with quivering
udders, they leap
over fences like sheep
you count. I still
haven't done the breakfast
dishes, although
I've been up for hours—
egg has congealed
on crockery, milk
has gone sour.

Meanwhile, wisteria
mounts the porch, pendulous
clusters swooning in gusts
of wind. It may rain

or not, maybe I'll wear
a sweater, but what if
later I'm too hot?

Down in the driveway
my old car
is spattered with droppings
of birds,
which flit around
in the bushes, presumably
unconcerned.

Black Spring

Charles Cantrell

When my father died I walked the railroad
where he fell. I walked one rail at least 100 feet
before I lost my balance. I did not stumble,
drunk, like my father. The parallel glare of iron
lifted the sun right into my eyes; they began to water.
I looked away and sprinted down the tracks
toward the rough field where my father and I
used to pick blackberries. In the field,
briars on scrubby bushes tore my trousers.
I wanted to fill my mouth with berries
until I couldn't talk, could hardly breathe
and let the juice run down like black blood,
my blood, more than I needed. Stuff it so far back
that it becomes sweet, letting, I hoped,
only good memories hang on, like those bristled nuggets
that burst in my mouth. In my haste I forgot
it was spring. Nothing but green berries,
no bigger than thimbles, and they hung tight.
I sat on a rock and imagined those berries turning
red then black, and how my father, in a hurry,
placed two cloths on both sides of each bush,
reached inside and shook the limbs for the loose

berries, then showed me how to lift the cloth
into a funnel for the pail.
On the rock I felt water pool
inside my mouth from those imaginary berries.

Sustenance

Christy Wise

As we pulled up to the giraffe preserve just outside Nairobi, my husband surveyed the tall, majestic giraffes in their 60-acre clearing, a compound designed to replicate the savannah of their natural habitat. I turned off the jeep's ignition and watched him take it all in as a child would: the two-story covered wooden platform circled by handrails where visitors stood eye-level with giraffes who were quite interested in the people with their hands full of pellets; the scrubby dirt clearing where the giraffes stood around in the hot sun when they weren't at the platform, gnawing on acacia leaves; and, beyond the clearing, the wild acreage with groves of Umbrella gum acacia trees, gum tree eucalyptus, Carissa bushes, and savannah grasses. This wasn't the expanse of the southern African savannah, but provided the components to the giraffes and offered humans a proximity to animals that they wouldn't experience in the wild or at most zoos.

In his faded work shirt and khakis, Bob looked quite different from his customary business attire of a shirt, tie, and gray suit. And his demeanor had changed. He was more relaxed and less distracted than back home in Washington, D.C. His forehead was free of the furrowed lines I often saw at the end of the day. Now, as he saw how close he could get to the giraffes, he smiled broadly.

"Let's go!" he said. "I can't wait."

We piled out of the jeep, bought pellets at the booth just inside the park, and then climbed the stairs to the platform, hearing the squeals of children who were feeding the giraffes. Not everyone on the platform was squealing: some people talked to giraffes as they held out their hands and others didn't feed giraffes at all, they simply watched. One little girl put her entire hand into a giraffe's mouth to give it the pellets.

"It's amazing to be here," Bob said, stopping to decide where he wanted to stand along the railing.

"I'm really glad we decided to come," I said.

We'd hesitated to visit the Langata Giraffe Centre for Rothschild giraffes because it sounded touristy and contrived, but we had extra time in Nairobi before beginning our safari and were eager to start seeing animals. Plus, we'd get much closer to giraffes here than in the wild, and certainly closer to a Rothschild, or Baringo giraffe, the most rare of the nine subspecies. Only a few hundred were left in the world, some in Kenya and others in Murchison Falls National Park in Uganda.

The Rothschild giraffe is named for Lord Walter Rothschild, British banker, politician and zoologist, who was the first to identify the Rothschild giraffe as a separate subspecies. In general, the Rothschild giraffes resemble other giraffe species with their long, spindly legs, their long necks, and their quilt-patched coat. With no markings below their knees, they seem to be wearing white stockings. Their coats are paler when compared to the Masai giraffe, and the patches are less jagged. Another key difference between them and other giraffe species is that they have five small horns, or ossicones, instead of two, which sounds a bit grotesque, but three of the horns are more like small bumps and not immediately visible. Two small horns are tucked behind the giraffes' ears, a small horn, or bump really, sits at the center of their foreheads, and two prominent horns project from the tops of their heads.

After finding an empty section of handrail, we stood looking out at the clearing, food ready. A tall giraffe ambled over from where he stood near a scrawny thorn acacia and stretched his neck toward us. Bob tentatively reached out his hand, gingerly pinching a couple of pellets between his forefinger and thumb, expecting to drop the pellets into the giraffe's mouth. The giraffe extended a huge blue-black tongue, longer than a banana though flat, like a banana cut in half lengthwise. Bob pulled back in surprise, clutching his hand to his chest. I laughed. Bob ignored me. He was ready to go again, this time with more resolve. He inched out his flat palm, now full of food, and the giraffe stretched forward again, and this time, as the giraffe's tongue extended, Bob held his arm steady and the giraffe scooped the pellets into his mouth. Bob smiled broadly and triumphantly. As the giraffe ate pellets from his right hand, Bob reached out his left hand, gently rubbing the giraffe's large forehead and long nose. Then, Bob puckered his lips and started cooing. The giraffe twitched its ears slightly, moving a little closer to Bob. The two of them entered into a small universe of their own, and, standing only a few steps away, I felt like a bit of an intruder.

"Oh, you sweet thing. Did you like that food?" Bob asked. Both of them held the exact same posture: neck stretched forward, head tilted up, lips puckered. One head was small, flesh-colored with brown hair, pursed lips, cooing and talking; the other head was large, brown and cream, with lips constantly moving in search of food. The giraffe looked at Bob through enormous dark brown eyes with long sweeping eyelashes and was silent except for crunching its food.

Bob reached into his bag for more pellets and he and the giraffe continued their conversation, with the giraffe eating and Bob talking. The skin above the giraffe's eyes was wrinkled, giving the animal a soulful look.

"Oh, you cute little baby," Bob said. "Your nose is so soft and your eyes are so big and brown." He stroked the giraffe's nose and forehead, occasionally offering pellets with his other hand. His affection for this animal that he'd never met before was basic, pure, and unselfconscious.

I looked around at other people feeding giraffes, and at other giraffes. Many people followed a pattern of reaching out to the animal, giving it food, and then pulling back suddenly when the giraffe stepped closer. In response, the giraffe pulled away. Then the humans stepped to the railing again and the dance started once more. Bob had moved beyond that duet. After his initial surprise, he was steadfast. He stretched out his hand full of food with a sense of purpose, didn't hesitate when the giraffe came to eat, and then reached out further toward the giraffe to pet it with his other hand, talking the whole time. Not only was he completely absorbed by feeding what had become his special giraffe, but he looked like he'd been doing this for years.

Gone was the rigidity of his life at home with its schedules, pressures, meetings, and formality. Gone were the boundaries that Bob placed between himself and others. He seemed to have forgotten where he was and even who he was in this conversation with his new friend. They each provided sustenance for the other, for one it was food and for the other, a deeper, more abstract type of sustenance. I almost didn't recognize my own husband.

Hopewell Junction

Jack Donahue

He stood there blowing hot air. *What a loudmouth blowhard*, I thought. He must have been born with a mini bullhorn organically grown into his larynx. Judging by his volume, the audience he hoped for was everyone in the waiting room. From what I observed from my seat opposite his, no one was listening except the elderly couple sitting right next to him. They were stuck real good, boxed in with no other seats to be had. It was late at night. The trains ran but once an hour. He wasn't saying anything threatening to them. If you took away the loud voice and analyzed what he was saying, the subject matter was actually kind of interesting. Not interesting to me and by the looks on the older couples' near-dead faces, there was little interest on their part. But someone somewhere could have been interested. Who knows? Every now and then, the woman would look directly at him and give him one of those painful half smiles out of politeness, I guess. He never once asked them a question about themselves. It was all about him.

I came in the middle of his oration and so at first thought those older folks were his relatives or even parents. He was going on and on about a cousin coming in from Colorado. He was going to show her the town because she's never been. But then I fell asleep for a few minutes and when I woke up, I swear to God there was a different older couple sitting in the exact same seats as the first pair and Mr. Self-Importance was still discoursing on his life and still waiting on his cousin from Colorado. Anyway, what he said next really threw me because I didn't know what the hell he was talking about. Therefore, I'm going to pull the curtain back a little bit, so to speak, and let you listen in on him yourselves as if you were sitting in the station, having just missed a train home and stuck right where I was with this windbag pontificating *ad nauseam*.

"I teach ESL because I have a gift for languages. I lived in China for several years, and spent about six years in the Czech Republic. Travelled throughout Europe and Asia. Lived in Russia and India for a while. Some of the African dialects are tricky, but after you live with the natives for a while you can pick them up somewhat." At this moment the little old lady leaned toward him as if to get in a word or two, if he would only shut up for two seconds. I don't know if the old man heard a word he said because he just stared straight ahead with somewhat of a half smile on his face. I don't know who or what he was looking at, if anything. Certainly not at me. Not anyone behind me or to the sides of me. The waiting room was packed. If he was staring at the wall there was nothing to look at except industrial gray paint and cheap aluminum molding. There was a map on the wall that looked kind of interesting, but he wasn't staring at that. I made a mental note to look at the map myself later on, once I could figure this guy out.

Anyhow, the lady almost fell on the floor, leaning over her husband, to get this guy to shut up for two seconds. He finally noticed her and this is what she said, "We were in Denver once. It was late at night and a big storm came in and they were about to shut the airport down but we got the last plane out of there. I've never slept in an airport before, and I never plan to."

That being said by the lady, the orator gives her a slight nod and jumps right back into what he was saying before the interruption: "My cousin should be coming in from Denver very soon. Anyhow, like I said I know many languages. I speak Korea fluently; a little Japanese, Italian...Italian is the most beautiful spoken language. With all the open vowels and how one word just flows into the next like a smooth, not-too-thick syrup being poured from one container to the next and nothing spilling over—just a nice, easy flow. Each word a poem. A thing of beauty. Something to linger on and savor. Whereas Japanese is an ugly language. It is harsh and ugly. That's all I got to say about that. But I speak it. I'd probably be able to speak it a little bit more if I didn't hate it so much. I'm not saying I hate the Japanese people. Don't get me wrong. I just don't like their language. Like I said, I speak a lot of Korea, probably because I lived there for so many years."

The guy stood up but continued to blow and blow from a standing position. Did you notice that twice he said "I speak Korea?" And the lady never corrected him. It's like if I said to someone, "I speak America" or "I speak Canada," the whole chorus of the full waiting room would have said "Hey stupid, America and Canada are countries, not languages." If he's got a gift for languages, how come he couldn't get that right?

Anyhow, I had enough of this guy and went over to look at the station map. As I walked past him, he didn't smell so good and his boots were scuffed. His jacket was too thin for this kind of weather, and his hair was all matted down and there were deep lines cut into his tanned face that I didn't notice at first. What do I care? I'm just killing time in the waiting room. I walked over to look at the map on the far wall, stepping over some outstretched legs and around cranky kids who were up way past their bedtimes. Maybe their parents took them to some show which they cared less about and would never remember anyway. What a waste of money. They should have saved their money and their time and just stayed home where it's warm. A lot of people underestimate that simple pleasure—staying home where it is nice and warm.

In any event, I got a close look at the map. I could see the date it was published at the bottom right hand corner, and man, was this in need of an update. It was brown with age and parts of it peeled back from the frame, but there was nothing else to look at. Despite the map's age, I was fascinated by the many lines thrusting out from the center of the city, spiking into all these different communities I never even knew existed, much less visited. The surface of it looked like the vein pattern on a slightly cracked egg—random, uneven, and going seemingly nowhere and everywhere at the same time. The perspective of the lines made it seem like toward the end of some of the routes some of the lines got thinner, disappearing into the point of infinity like they teach you in art class. By the way, it was an electric map. Not all the bulbs worked, but I guess the original intention was for the train passenger to see at a glance the progress of her train coming in and what stop it was at along the way. But mostly, the only bulbs left were the last stops on each line so you didn't know where the hell your train was or if it was stuck or derailed or whatever. I looked at the names of the stops. Some of them I recognized and some were just names of areas in various towns and villages: Pond Reserve; Ringgold; Two Daughters; Elderville; Bottom Green; Hopewell Junction. That has a nice ring to it. Hopewell Junction. I hope everyone is well in Hopewell Junction.

It got quiet all of a sudden. What I would call peace. The blowhard must've been resting his vocal chords for a few seconds. Even blowhards need to catch their breath so they can create the next imaginary moment of their pathetic lives. I turned around so I could see what he looked like with his mouth closed. He wasn't there and half the place emptied out. So I ran down the stairs and jumped into the first car I could, with the doors closing behind me. No more last call, all aboard. You're on your own in this city. The train had ten or twelve cars so it absorbed a lot of bodies. Only two or three other people were in my car as far as I could tell. I couldn't see everyone. Some people slump down and take up all four seats like it's their private slumber car or something. Probably so few people in this car because it had a bathroom. You'd think that at least one of the passengers would just pull the bathroom door shut as they came in so it wouldn't stink so much for them and everyone else. Piss on the floor. Piss all over the raised seat and toilet paper rolling on the floor. Some people are pigs. Their mamas never taught them bathroom manners. They're probably pigs at home too. But who wants to even go into a car like that? No, they'd rather just flop and go to sleep in three seconds, then miss their stop forty minutes later, call their wives and say *could you pick me up* at whatever the last stop was. So the wife would have to drive in her pajamas and bathrobe to pick the lazy bastard up. How some people stay married is beyond me. I shut the door, sat in the middle of the car and said to myself *shut up*. I'm going on and on just like the blowhard waiting for his cousin from Colorado, even if it's only in my mind that I'm ranting. I should just thank God for my blessings. *Thank you God for giving me such a stinking life. Merry Christmas to you, too.*

Anyhow, I'm glad I made the train. Usually I like to get to a train a few minutes early. I like to walk the whole stretch of the platform so I could feel the hard bumps of the yellow rubber warning mat on the soles of my feet. It's like a free massage. I didn't even care where this train was going. If the weatherman was right for once, it could be the last train out of the city tonight. And I needed to get the hell out of the city. I couldn't stand it anymore. Everything's going to shut down if the big storm they are predicting actually comes this way. A blizzard's coming, no two ways about it. I hate the way they report the weather these days. They give you the wind chill factor on top (or below) the temperature. Just give me the damn temperature, will you, just like they did in the old days. I'll figure out how cold I feel all by myself. They must want to rationalize their meteorological degrees or the big pay they get. That's the job I want, weatherman. That or a government economist. Either one would work for me. Right or wrong, you still get paid. Best two jobs in America in my opinion.

As soon as the train came out of the tunnel I knew they were right this time. This would definitely be the last train tonight. The wind and snow just smacked that double thick glass and chased me to the outside seat. As soon as I switched to the aisle I couldn't believe my eyes. Here he comes, the blowhard, walking right toward me and it was too late to slink into oblivion. Maybe he's on the prowl for another old couple who can absorb one of his grandiose lectures.

Oh no. Too late. Eye contact made. He stands right over me. I can see close up in the harsh light that his fingernails are long and filthy, as if he scraped grime off a car engine or worked with dirty machinery and never washed his hands. The skin of his face was his worst feature. Tanned, but not a healthy beach tan. A beaten-by–the-wind tan. Too many lines and furrows. His hair was greased back but not handsome slick like Robert Redford in *The Great Gatsby*. This guy needed a good scrub down. The low light he had in the waiting room was his best friend.

"You got a ticket?" he asked, standing right above me. I could smell a trace of cheap booze on his breath.

"Why, you the conductor?" I challenged him. He didn't answer me right away but just stared at me. A penetrating, too-intimate stare. I didn't want to mess with this guy. He was big and looked like he didn't give a shit if he lived or died. I guessed that he'd fight to the death if he had to, and for no good or noble reason.

"You got a ticket or not?" he demanded.

"No," I said, "I didn't have time to get one."

He takes a crumpled paper out of his pants pocket and hands it me. "This is a ten-tripper and it's got one trip left on it. It's for a different line, but that doesn't matter. They have to give you some credit based on zones," he said in a voice much lower than his waiting room voice. I took the ticket from his filthy hand. He left his hand extended so I could shake it. I thought he'd have a much stronger grip but I was surprised how soft and gentle it was. A caress almost. "Where are you headed?" he wanted to know but I wasn't about to get personal with a stranger, so I just shrugged my shoulders. I only wished I could sprout wings and escape this tight trap but he might follow me from one car to the next. Like those two older couples in the waiting room, I was now his captive audience.

Instead of asking me again where I was headed, he offered me some free advice. "Listen, we all got stories," he said in a whisper, looking down the aisle to see if the conductor was anywhere in sight. He then leans closer to me and his breath is a mix of wine, beer, and smoke. "Don't get off at Hopewell Junction tonight. Just go to the end of the line."

"Why are you telling *me* this?" I asked. His stare shot right through me, "We all got stories, buddy. You got a story. I got a story. My story is probably pretty close to yours. Had a job. Lost a job. Then the bitch kicked me out. Blah, blah, blah. What does it matter?"

"Why the end of the line?" I had to know. What's his reasoning? Then he started rocking a little bit. I thought he was going to fall right into my lap and I'd never get him off.

"Just go to the end of the line," he insisted, "Jimmy's the maintenance guy on duty tonight. He leaves the waiting stall open. And he keeps the heat on all night. I swear he's going to get fired soon but he's got a heart for guys like you and me."

You and me? I thought to myself. *So now we belong to the same club?*

"Jimmy isn't much of a janitor and the stall smells like piss but it's our piss, if you know what I mean," he says straight out. "Anyhow, what you can do is stay there all night and you'll be warm. If you see Jimmy, just tell him you met Butch."

Okay. Now the blowhard has an identity. His name is Butch. What kind of name is that for a professor of Italian, and some Chinese and Korea? He speaks Korea, I reminded myself, and that made me feel a little better about the company I was keeping.

"Why shouldn't I stop at Hopewell Junction?" I asked.

"It's locked up tight," Butch advised, "you'll freeze your ass off there. But you want to stop there in the morning."

"Why?" I had to know.

"Stay at the end of the line until the sun comes up. You'll want to get out of there before the commuters start to come in numbers. Someone'll complain and ruin it for Jimmy. Ruin it for Jimmy, and you ruin it for the rest of us."

"The rest of us?" I inquired.

Butch didn't answer me but just took a deep breath and the breeze of all that wine, beer, and smoke attacked my nostrils. Better than smelling salts, and it lingers. I was no longer tired. I was into this guy's lecture. Now the wind really picks up and bangs against the window with a big, powerful fist. I could see the snow drifts building in a hurry.

Butch catches my eye, "This one's a killer."

"I hope not," is my answer. "Where are you getting off?

"Hopewell Junction." Before I could ask him why, he simply says, "I got some business there tonight, but you do as I tell you and you'll survive the night. Come back to Hopewell Junction in the AM, a little past daybreak. Go down the escalator and speak to Steve. That's his sandwich truck you'll see at the base of the escalator. Go up to him and tell him Butch is your friend."

Now Butch is my friend. And I thought I just wanted to be alone tonight.

Butch continues, "Don't go up to him when there's a lot of customers around. Wait until he's got a little bit of a lapse and make sure you mention my name. He'll give you a black coffee and a cheese Danish. That'll hold you for awhile. Later on, I'll tell you what stations are good for a sandwich or soup or..." This time Butch did keel over. Right into the seats across the aisle. He got up almost immediately and looked straight ahead. He spoke quickly, "Listen. The conductor's on his way. Just give him the ticket I gave you. I got to move along, but some other time I'll tell you which stations are good for food, washing up, pitching for money, all that good stuff you've got to get to know especially on nights like this."

"How are we supposed to meet up with each other?" I asked.

"Here's my business card," he laughs as he hands me an empty chewing gum wrapper from his pocket. "Just call me at my office and my secretary will tell you how to get a hold of me. Or call me on my cell. Better yet, email me. I always answer my emails." He looks down the aisle again and offers this last bit of advice: "Tomorrow, when you come back from the end of the line, the conductor on the six o'clock train is an idiot. Just tell him anything that pops into your head. What works best is you tell him you got beat up and the mugger took all of your money and your monthly pass. Got it?"

"Got it," I said as Butch left my side just as the conductor came into our car.

"We'll see each other again, don't worry about that," he said as he hurried into the next car.

I called out to him, "Did your cousin from Colorado ever show up?"

"Nah. She owes me a lot of money. I don't ever expect to see her again as long as I live," he boomed in his waiting room voice.

The conductor took my ticket; no questions asked. I rode to the end of the line and slept where Butch told me to sleep. As it turns out, the storm wasn't as bad as they predicted. The sun was just coming up and I could see down to the streets. The heavy salters and plows were chugging along one after the other, not meeting much resistance. It was freezing though and when I see Butch next, I'll ask him where I could get some gloves and maybe a heavy blanket.

I got off the train at Hopewell Junction and saw some commotion at the bottom of the escalator.

As I rode down I could see the commuters using the up escalator as a staircase because it wasn't moving. They looked even unhappier than me. How bad could it be that they had to climb upstairs. Lazy bastards. In a way I'm glad I'm not a commuter anymore.

As I got closer to the bottom, I saw the sandwich truck but there was a lady pouring the coffee, handing out donuts, and making change. She didn't look like any kind of Steve to me. When I got to the bottom, I could see the up escalator making one false start after another, clicking and clucking in the rhythm of a big mechanical zipper stuck in hopeless monotony. People were all sorts of pissed off. No free ride this morning.

I could see there was something stuck in the bottom step of the escalator. A big piece of thick cloth all bunched up, mucking up the gears. Then, off to the side, I saw where the piece of cloth came from. People were stepping over what looked like the body of a man. The bare skin of his pale left leg was exposed to the freezing cold. There were traces of dried blood on his leg.

I walked around the sandwich cart to get a closer look at the body on the ground. The man wore a thin black vinyl jacket and cargo pants. The piece of cloth sticking in the gears of the escalator came right off that man's pants. I knew it was Butch but I didn't know if he was alive or dead.

"Where's Steve?" I asked the sandwich truck lady.

"Who's Steve?" she answered as she made change for a twenty.

"The guy who owns the sandwich truck," I said.

"I own this truck," the lady said defiantly. "You must be talking about the guy who used to have this route."

Now I'm getting a little excited as the commuters continue to step over Butch's body to catch their trains. "What about this guy on the ground? Anybody call for help?" I demanded.

"Listen buddy. I got a business to run," she said. "Besides, that guy doesn't need any help right now."

"Why not?" I asked, wondering if this whole scene was real or some kind of cruel fantasy.

"He's gone," she said as another customer took her coffee and cheese Danish and stepped over Butch. Yet another customer came up to the lady and asked "When's the mechanic coming to fix the escalator? Do you know?"

I knelt down to look at Butch. There was a pool of liquid that spilled out of his mouth. It iced up like a little skating rink beneath his dark face. One side of his face lay flat on the ground. His flesh sealed itself to the cement. Man and ground were one with each other.

The trains ran on time this morning. Steam flowed out of each cup of hot chocolate and coffee. I suppose people got to their offices on time. I suppose that the heat came up from the boiler rooms in most of the office buildings. And surely there was an ample supply of liquid soap in the bathroom dispensers and back-up toilet paper in each one of the stalls. By the time I left Hopewell Junction, things were almost back to normal. Some kind of official vehicle loaded up Butch's body. I didn't watch how they got his face off the frozen ground. They put his big body in a plastic bag and that was it. The coffee lady had a good morning. Sales were strong.

If Butch were still around he could have told me about the Ringgold station. I wonder if that stop is good for anything. Now I have to find out for myself. What happened with all of Butch's knowledge, I wondered. All that knowledge of languages and whatever else he knew. Now that he is dead, does it go with him wherever he's headed for all eternity? Is it packed tightly in his brain like a compressed file on a jump drive? What happens to all of that? Maybe the good news is that it stays with the people he taught. That's if what he told those old folks was actually true. Seeing his body on the ground and a piece of his cargo pants stuck in the escalator wasn't the most pleasant sight I've ever beheld. I plan to fight to stay alive today and I have to admit I'm a little bit scared. Too bad Butch didn't live another day. I guess we could have been real friends. He had a lot more to tell me. I don't really know if he had all the language skills he bragged about or if he could even speak one word of Korea. But I do know two things for sure: The ticket he gave me was good and I didn't freeze to death last night. Second, and most importantly, he did teach me about the end of the line. He sent me to a place where I would be warm. At least for last night. Tonight's another story.

7 Mini Fictions

Greg Evason

1. Once upon a time.
2. Benjamin Brat found his socks.
3. It was the last day of winter and Samantha Stone.
4. The town was located halfway between boredom and a rigorous canoe.
5. Mrs. Brown stood staring out the kitchen window at the big black birds and she knew this meant some poems were on their way.
6. It was today.
7. A long time ago.

Venezia, Last Visit With Peggy Guggenheim

Karol M. Wasylyshyn

In the palazzo courtyard
There
sudden words seen
living on the surface of
a stone:

Savor kindness
Because
Cruelty is
Always
Possible later.

Was it there
There
that I saw your
most
serious
…reflection?

Eastward Ho

Dorthea Balabus

3,000 miles of railroad track,
five days of wondrous scenery, five nights of being lulled to sleep by a
    clacking rhapsody.

Oceans, rivers, deserts and streams.
Bridges that echo, napping at will.

Watching children make knitted tube rugs to while away the hours.
Buttermilk pancakes, hot cocoa, first cup of coffee aroma, awakens me
    from the railroad sleeping cocoon.

Each state proudly welcoming the El Capitan Cross Country Flyer,
    showing off its landscape and ever changing skies.

The Darwinian Co-op Lending Library

Vivian Lawry

We have all these people waiting in line, see, because we always have long lines for the holidays, and I have to tell this woman all the turkey basters are out. So she just goes off on me, like, "What kind of a lending library is this? First you don't have a meat grinder and now no turkey baster?"

I'm like, "I'm sorry, ma'am, but you have to request meat grinders through inter-library loan."

And then she goes, "That's no excuse for the turkey baster!"

I'm like, "It's five o'clock on Christmas Eve, ma'am. All the turkey basters are out."

And she goes, "I've belonged to the Friends of the Library for thirty years, and this is the treatment I get? Who do you think donated the Santa suit, Bozo, the scuba-diving equipment—not to mention red sheets and heart pillows for roll-away beds. Just see if I donate anything else!"

Everyone behind her shifts from foot to foot and rolls their eyes, trying to balance punchbowls and tinsel and stuff. But co-ops run on donations. The head librarian invites her to have a cup of tea, says she could check out a nice lemon zester, or a fish poacher. I think the old days I've heard about, when people borrowed books and seldom came in around the holidays, weren't so bad. But once we started lending tapes and CDs and children's puzzles, there was no turning back.

The next person in line's a repeater. This is his third year checking out a puppy on Christmas Eve. He'll renew for a second two weeks, until his kids shirk their puppy chores. Word's out about our pet collection—we do a brisk business in rabbits and chicks for Easter—but puppies are tops. So I hand over the collie mix, yap-yap-yapping and wiggling his butt. The man says, "Do you have a Goldendoodle? The kids would like a Goldendoodle this year."

I'm like, "This is our last puppy."

He eyes the wriggling furball and goes, "How about tropical fish? Or a bear cub? Hey, I've got it. A de-scented skunk. That would be really festive."

So finally I'm like, "We've had a run on pets. It's either this puppy or a cat, your choice." He reaches for the puppy. No one ever checks out a cat.

We expected the run on pets. But the really hot item—totally took us by surprise—has been kids. Preschoolers, mostly, old enough not to wet the bed and young enough to be cute, suitable for photos and not too picky about presents. The parents who donate them mostly head someplace warm, and require a two-week-minimum loan. I turn to the couple picking up twins, and slide the informed consent form across the counter. The little girl says, "We get Cocoa Puffs for breakfast and Coke before we go to bed." The boy kicks the man in the shins. I'm like, "Read the parts about allergies and bedtime snacks carefully before you sign them out."

Then this woman rushes in, navy banker suit and pearls, and barges in front of the line. I think there'll be a blow-up. But everyone just stands there while she goes, "I need a family."

I'm like, "You need to wait your turn."

She goes, "I don't have time to wait. My parents called from the airport—'Surprise, we're here for Christmas with you and Joe and the kids.' I never thought this would happen, never in a million years." She leans closer and lowers her voice. "Look, years ago I told them I eloped, to keep them off my back. Then they wanted grandkids, so I made some up. But now they're here, and I've got to have a family for Christmas!" Someone behind her snickers. She blushes. "Surely you have one. I only need one."

I go, "You are so in luck. We have a father with three kids left."

She looks startled when they come out. Then she laughs, tucks a blond curl behind her ear, and goes, "Perfect! I don't even have to make up a reason for keeping them apart, for not sending pictures." She laughs again and leaves, arm in arm with the tall black father, the three kids trailing like ducklings.

Someone says, "What kind of woman would lend her husband and kids over Christmas?"

And I'm like, "Lots of Jewish families are okay with it. And single-parent families. And sometimes psychotherapists. Therapists are really pressed for time around the holidays."

The next woman leans in and goes, "I reserved the Chinese grandparents." As if I'd asked, she goes, "My children need exposure to Mandarin before we visit the homeland—and to the whole female subservience thing."

So I'm like, "Whatever." I run her card, hand her the due date slip. "Remember, back by Boxing Day or you incur huge fines. Merry Christmas."

A teenage girl edges up to the counter, eyes skittering sideways, and whispers, "I don't really need to check out a whole person. I just need—you know—parts."

I stifle a laugh. I'm like, "What exactly do you need?"

She glances at her flat chest and goes, "I need a couple of pounds of body fat—just 'til after New Years."

I print her due date slip. IMHO, body parts are going to be our next high-demand items.

I glance at the clock. Nearly six. A short man in a black coat and homburg steps forward and goes, "Do you honor cards from other libraries?"

I'm like, "We have reciprocal agreements with all the regional libraries."

He goes, "Great! I want a book—'*Twas the Night Before Christmas*."

I don't know what to say, so I'm like, "Let me check with the head librarian."

The head librarian goes, "I'm sure we have a copy somewhere. Let me check the antiquities index." She heads off at a half trot, the man in the homburg hard on her heels.

The clock strikes six and I'm like, "Yes." I leave her to it, check out my own two pounds of body fat and my escort for *The Nutcracker*, and head home for the holidays.

Bernie's Cancer

Dr. William Miller

He brought it back
from Vietnam,
on a boat filled
with boys fresh from
rice paddies mined
with trip wire explosives.

He fell in love
with my ex-wife,
moved in with her
and my son, took them
out on weekends
for pizza and cold beer.

One night he woke
from a dream of a
noisy hospital tent,
a fine white mist
that powdered
acres of jungle leaves.

The first doctor
told him it was just
a scratch and would heal
inside a week;
the second said he had
less than a year.

My son almost cried
when he told me the news:
he loved the man
who told the best stories
of a country alive
with tree snakes.

And when he died,
I didn't know
how to grieve for
my son, the soldier
whose hand I shook
only once, an ex-wife
I still loved.

Break Up

H.D. Brown

i don't care if you leave me
i'm doin' wife work for girlfriend wages anyway
she shouted

she didn't actually
it would have made me stay

Waterfall

Phyllis Grilikhes

Words shine through
a splash of falling water
bits of meaning
tumble over rocks
splatter at your feet
wait to be claimed
before they vanish
into the pulsing course
hidden—
forever nameless
in the watery spread

Gyr

Kevin Breen

On the first evening of a backpacking trip in the mountains, Tommy Flynn slips away from camp, drawn by a shaft of sunlight striking a granite escarpment. He jumps a small stream and begins climbing to the radiant ridge. Maneuvering around shrubs and boulders, he smells spruce trees, sage, and other aromas too faint to make out. The idea of becoming an animal for a day, a bear maybe, roaming the high-country and smelling the information-packed air, excites him. At the top, sweat moistening his forehead and struggling to breathe, he peers five-hundred feet down to the tiny tents of his group in shadow, clustered among the burnt yellows and umbers of the autumnal valley. Up high, at 10,000 feet, a honeyed light still warms the land.

Flynn wanders forward onto the plateau until he can see into another valley.

"Hey," he hears a perturbed whisper. "Get down."

A girl sits on a fallen tree, binoculars to her eyes, focused on a spot in the secluded valley. He crouches beside her. She must be the lone figure he spotted several times earlier on the hike in, walking on a ridge paralleling the trail.

"Elk," she says, not turning, speaking softly. "Been watching this cow for an hour. She's about three or four, coming into her best years. Something of a loner. But content. Ruminating. It's a good night to be an elk."

Her voice, tangy with some smooth friction in it, appeals to him. A tangled mass of dark hair bunches around her shoulders over a hooded sweatshirt. Lying beside her in a leather sheath is a Bowie knife.

"She's grazing on the tenderest grasses and mountain sorrel, straying from the herd. She's a brave one, but still she sniffs the air, looking around, listening. For bear or cougar, or men, but she feels good. Minimal worries. Sometimes she glances at the bull and feels that crazy urge to have him ride her. But she's not in estrus. Not yet."

In the distant valley Flynn sees several tan spots, the size of mice. "Are you a biologist?"

She lowers the binoculars and turns toward him, nodding. "Kinda... Not really... No." Her lips scrunch lopsidedly and her brow furrows. Her round face contains rosy cheeks, a slightly upturned nose, a pink mouth with complicated, curvy lips, and pointy teeth. Her eyes, catching the sun's final rays, are maple brown, shiny, as though shellacked.

"What's your name?"

"Gyr," she says, looking away.

"Jeer?"

"Like the raptor. Gyrfalcon."

"Gyr?" he says again, not getting it. "Gyrfalcon?"

He sees her look at him—registering his short brown hair and thin face, the bright blue coat, the new green hiking pants—like he's less interesting than an elk pellet. "Let me guess," she says. "Joey? Timmy? Tommy?"

Flynn, he says, thinking a second too late he should have made up a name. Wolf. Or Panther. No doubt what she had done—her real name's probably Sue or Ashley. He tells her that he will be doing the 50-mile Crest Trail, along with nine other hikers.

She sneers, as though she has just tasted road kill. "Ten people? It's like a parade or a marching band. Are you the tuba player?"

He asks her what her plans are and she says she has enough food for a week. She might make it to Lake Solitude in the north, but who knows.

"No plan is the best plan, my Daddy always said."

The sun has burrowed itself at the horizon and the first star gleams in a purple ceramic sky. The bull elk calls, like a squealing flute on its highest octave. Gyr brings the binoculars to her eyes again, a misty breath showing in front of her.

"Elk see well in the darkness," she murmurs. "Better than us. More rods, less cones. They don't see color very good. They have panoramic vision and are aware of everything. They probably smell us up here." She puts the glasses down and brings a pretend rifle up to her shoulder, and says, ambivalently, "Even so, I could drop her if I had my Remington 30-06."

He tells her he should be getting back, that he didn't bring a flashlight, and she shrugs. He walks past a sleeping bag spread out on a tarp on the grass, a medium-sized pack beside it, feeling a surge of jealousy at the girl's independence. What would it be like to be alone in the mountains for a week? Would his mind wander down new paths? He scrambles down the ridge, crosses the stream, and heads to his tent where he is stopped by the group's leader, Aaron, a man with wavy brown hair and thick thighs squeezed into spandex pants. His arms are folded over his broad chest, and a silver whistle, attached to a purple cord, dangles below his neck.

"Leaving camp without telling anyone?" he says, in a high-pitched voice. "No water. No whistle. No flashlight. Probably not a good idea."

Flynn says sure, no problem.

"If you feel the urge to wander off," Aaron says, "at least let me know where you are going."

Flynn walks to his tent and slips into his sleeping bag, content as darkness falls to be back among the group. He misses his nice home on Lake Michigan and the king-size bed, his yellow Lab, Beston, and Zandra, his fiancé, whom he will marry in two months. She encouraged him to go on this trip, buying him the new clothes, a pretty sky-blue water bottle, a two-pound utensil set.

"Go for it," she said. "Find some gorp-eating weirdoes like yourself. Just, *please* don't ask me to go camping."

He drifts off to sleep thinking about the furniture company and lumberyard he recently took over from his father. When he wakes during the night, the young woman alone on the plateau, sleeping under the stars, sparks an envy so sharp it keeps him awake till dawn. In the cool darkness he wonders about many things: why the girl interests him so, why he is drawn to the wilderness when so many others aren't, why he and his father have never understood one another.

Steam rises from cups of coffee and tea and bowls of oatmeal—what some have begun to call gruel—in the chilly morning. They all gather around the kitchen area to eat and talk. At twenty-seven, Flynn is the youngest in the group—the rest are in their forties or fifties and are veterans of group hikes. Until now, Flynn has only hiked in the Midwest, and he is the only one who has not been above 10,000 feet, the altitude of most of the Crest Trail. The others refer to him as the rookie or greenhorn.

Sitting on a log, Flynn eats his oatmeal and dried fruit and listens. He is a bit disappointed that there are no young women in the group, someone with whom he might flirt with, or maybe more. They are all doctors, lawyers, professors, and successful businessmen who talk about other trips they have taken around the world: dining on salmon steaks, fresh vegetables cooked in butter, and Tiramisu on the Haute Route in Switzerland; rafting the Copper River in Alaska, eating scrambled eggs and Hollandaise sauce and blueberry pancakes for breakfast. They joke about the food on this trip, one woman saying it isn't bad "if you were a flea-bitten, starving, ravenous dog."

Danny, the cook, a tall, lean man with a face as narrow as a collie's, cleans up, banging the pots and pans around and joking with the others. "This is what you eat on a real backpacking trip." A grimy chuckle works its way out of a half-grin. "By the fifth day, you'll all be asking for my recipes."

An hour later, as the sun spreads over camp, Flynn realizes the rest of the group is packed and eager to go, while he has his gear lying in piles around him. He tells Aaron, who is ready and waiting.

"Well, okay," Aaron says. "You can catch up. We will stop for lunch in four miles at Marion Lake. You can't miss it. You'd have to try to get lost. Listen for my whistle."

Aaron blows the whistle and leads the group out of the valley. Flynn packs his gear, remembering a dark-haired woman he met recently in a bar: "Don't let my big tits scare you," she said, by way of introduction, "I'm really a nice girl." Then he thinks of Zandra lying naked in his bed, her marigold hair splayed onto her shoulders, the morning light off Lake Michigan streaming through the bay windows and the hibiscus flowers. Through quivering pine needles, he spies movement coming down the slope. That odd-looking young woman. Gyr. She takes off her pack about 150 yards from him, fills her water bottle from the stream and strips off three or four layers of clothes and bathes in the shallow water.

She dresses and moves to the kitchen area with its packed-down grass and plops down, completely still. Flynn walks to where she is lying on her side, staring intently.

"What are you doing?"

"Ants," she says.

He looks closer and sure enough she is beside a teeming ant hole and red ants are scampering over the ground.

"I'm trying to think like an ant," she adds.

Flynn stares at her, perplexed, and then squints at the insects. "They can't be doing a whole lot of thinking, can they?"

"I've been following this one." She points to an ant hauling a crumb in its jaws. "She came out of the hole over here, and then wandered around like a drunk trying to find her car, until she happened upon part of your mob's breakfast. That's when it gets interesting. Instead of retracing her path back to the hole, she made a beeline back to it. How do you suppose she did that?"

Flynn gets on his knees and watches the ant approach the hole, enter abdomen first, and drag the big crumb down with her. If only his employees at the lumberyard worked half as hard. "Not a clue."

She explains, slowly, as though he might be a bit dense, that the ant isn't following a scent trail. She actually has some kind of crude cognitive map of the area in her head. Dead reckoning. Maybe she can identify landmarks, a grain of sand with a dent in the side. A piece of grass with a mold stain on it. Or the ant is attuned to the sun and its angle and can follow an azimuth by the time of the day.

"Her head is wired in some way that ours aren't. She might not have the impressive ability to watch *Gilligan's Island* re-runs for hours, or to drive a car into a ditch while yakking on a cell phone. But she does all right."

An image pops into his head of Zandra speeding down High-way 22 along Lake Michigan in her yellow Mercedes, chatting on her purple phone, a cup of Starbucks coffee in her holder, a CD of Alanis Morissette playing low: "*Do I stress you out?*" Beston rides shotgun, head out the window, grinning, smelling sand and fresh water, the remains of fish on the beach.

Her Daddy, Gyr says, wrinkles forming in her forehead, watched ants for hours, performing experiments. Picking them up and moving them five feet, then ten feet, then twenty feet away from their holes, to see if they could find their way back.

"He did other things, too," she says, gazing off toward the stream, blowing a shock of wayward hair from her eyes. "Like take a magnifying glass and burn them on a hot day. Watching them curl up and die. As a little girl, I'd hear their screams in my dreams. Or throw the ants into a spider's web and watch the spider mummify them and suck their fluids out. He liked to draw blood, that one."

Flynn feels disoriented, not sure if they are talking about animals or Gyr's father or something else altogether. Then she goes distant, in a sort of trance, as though she's figuring out some intricate problem. He thanks her for the science lesson and says goodbye, but she just stares at the ground, at something Flynn can't see.

Flynn proceeds across the gentle ridges and open meadows of the range. From high spots on the trail, he glimpses lofty peaks to the north and the group far ahead of him, their clothes flashy in the alpine brilliance. Squiggly black lines, like loose hairs, swim in his vision whenever he looks up at the bright blue sky. He stays behind, thinking about home and the company. How does this moment compare with selling a custom-made bookcase for $4,000? Not well, he's sure his father would answer.

An hour later, two faint whistle blasts—Aaron's signal for lunch—arrive on the thin breeze. They sit near the water, in the frail shade of stunted pine trees, eating Havarti cheese, Ritz crackers and summer sausage, washed down by the icy lake water. The conversation remains connected to the world below: jobs, homes, cars, wives and husbands. Only Aaron, a basketball and football referee, and Danny, a Canadian who never says what he does back home, focus on what is around them now.

When it is Flynn's turn to talk, he finds he is as bad as the rest. He tells them about the family business, and jokingly complains about running the company, the responsibility, the challenges, his father still coming to work every day even though he is retired. He downplays the benefits of his position: the money flowing into his bank account, the contemporary house on Lake Michigan, the fancy meals in restaurants, the attention of a woman like Zandra. Nor does he mention that sometimes he finds his father sitting in his office in a suit and tie with nothing to do, and he feels sorry for the old man.

The group climbs above timberline, through the aqua-tinted, lucent light of late afternoon. Their sounds—the chatter, the click of titanium walking sticks in the dirt and stones, the swish of nylon fabric—disperse into the open landscape. Everyone's tenacious grip on the world below gradually loosens, it seems. Flynn lets go of nice meals, watching Tigers baseball at night on his flat-screen TV, sleeping in his bed under the skylight. Aaron points out wildflowers—paintbrush, yellow cinquefoil, alpine avens—and landmarks: Spearhead Peak to the right, Fossil Mountain to the left. One woman talks about the colors and textures of cirrus clouds. Danny identifies the toot of a red-breasted nuthatch, the keening of a Red-tailed Hawk. Others discuss the geology of the mountains, the lichens growing on the exposed peaks. They break at the pass and no one speaks. In one direction, a trail winds down the forested Death Canyon to the broad lowlands and the river valley, back to towns and highways and roads and sidewalks. The other direction affords a view of mountain peak after mountain peak, fading into a silvery-blue background, heading toward the Yellowstone Mountains and the Yukon and the high Arctic.

They camp on the southern edge of a walled formation known as Death Canyon Shelf. The conversation picks up again. Voices ricochet off the wall as though twenty or thirty people are talking at once, jangling Flynn's nerves like a saw cutting into hardwoods—a sound his father once told him was the sound of money, sweeter than a Beethoven symphony. Flynn stays removed from the group, still enthralled by the vision of the untrammeled high-country, wanting to hold on to it. He pictures Gyr, tiny as a bird in the sky, plotting her peculiar course through this immensity.

The next day, a layover day, Aaron announces that he will lead a group down into Death Canyon, to look for wildlife and to explore the area. Everyone decides to go with Aaron, except Danny who says he will stay behind to meditate and work on his signature meal: angel hair pasta and Alfredo sauce and strawberry cheesecake. And Flynn, who says he will just hang close to camp.

After the group leaves, Flynn moseys down the trail they hiked yesterday, scanning the horizon, and finally admitting to himself that he is searching for Gyr. Back at Marion Lake, he stops for lunch beneath the stand of pines. The day is sunny and mild. The warmth makes him drowsy and he falls asleep to a boyhood memory: playing with friends, pretending he was a lion or a tiger or, his favorite, a black jaguar, roaming the humid light of the shadowy jungle.

When he wakes, Gyr is sitting beside him, hands around her knees, concentrating on a rock pile fifty feet away. Her homely petiteness, a kinetic tension in her muscles, and a detectable whiff of promiscuity electrifies his flesh for a quick, fierce moment.

"Weasel," she says. He frowns, wondering if she reads minds, until he follows her gaze. "If you keep still he might come out."

Flynn stares at the rocks, not moving. He has never seen a weasel in the wild before.

"What's it like," Gyr whispers—a puff of apple-scented breath tickling his ear—"to have four paws, a tail, to live in a hole in the ground lined with pika fur, littered with mice skulls? No TV. No lights. Heart thumping 150 beats a minute."

A sleek animal with brown fur and a lemon-colored belly ventures out of the rocks, peering at them with beady black eyes, its black nose twitching.

"What does he see?" Gyr prods. "What does he smell? What does he feel?"

Flynn concentrates, trying to make the leap from terra firma to terra incognita. "We are in his domain. He's annoyed. He wants us to leave. He's got big plans today, killing mice and pikas. Juicy beetles."

While Gyr's glossy brown eyes are locked on the weasel, Flynn marvels at what he has stumbled upon: a wild girl of the mountains raised by a crazy father. His own father would dismiss her as a grubby, irrelevant oddball, part of the lunatic fringe.

Gyr remains guru-still, until the weasel backs into his hole.

"It's cozy in there for him," she says. "Safe. He's looking out from the darkness, at the tiny hole of light. Then he curls up, closes his eyes, sleeping. Weasel dreams." An icy intensity builds in her gaze. "Some people would want to go in after him. To kill him, for sport.

For fun. To possess his perfect soul for their own twisted entertainment."

She glances at Flynn out the corner of one eye and then stands and slips on her pack. She studies a topographic map rubber-banded to her wrist, reads a bearing from a compass strapped like a watch to her other wrist, and takes off climbing up to the grassy meadow near the pass, avoiding the trail. Flynn follows, asking questions.

She has lived in Wyoming all of her life. Starting as a young girl, she was taken all over the state by her Daddy.

"We traveled cross-country, by map and compass. I've been in most of the ranges. Medicine Bow. The Winds. The Tetons. The Bighorns. The Laramie Range. The Sherman Mountains. The Yellowstones and the Absorakas. If there are grizzlies, I won't go there by myself. Grizzlies, I'm disappointed to admit, truly freak me out."

Lake Solitude is the southern limit of the grizzlies' range in these mountains.

Her Daddy, just before she was born, bought a gyrfalcon, a protected species, illegal as hell to own. "He always had pets. Dogs and cats. Foxes and ferrets. Raccoons. The day I was born, the gyrfalcon flew away when he was in the Bighorn foothills. He was teaching it to hunt, but the first time he let it loose it flew away, straight to the Arctic no doubt. A lot of his life was like that, things flying away from him. My mother, for one. For all we know, she's in the Arctic, too."

She sticks her tongue out at the piece of jerky Flynn is gnawing on and sinks her sharp, crooked teeth into an apple.

"He had photos," Gyr continues, "of the animals he had killed over thirty years. Him in camo, beside a dead elk slumped on the ground, its neck limp as a noodle; him with a turkey, its eyes dead as buttons; him with twenty trout dangling on a stringer. A brace of pheasants he had killed. Harmless snakes, songbirds, hawks, turtles and frogs. As a girl, I went hunting with him and quickly learned to kill. I was lethal. Daddy was so proud."

They walk in silence for a half an hour, a few mares' tails drifting over the mountains, Gyr taking occasional sightings from her compass.

Flynn begins to ask why her father didn't come on this trip, but the question is interrupted by a coyote's crazy howl. Flynn follows Gyr up a mountain and at the summit they gaze out over a rocky landscape riddled with small lakes, meandering streams, and stunted pine trees, all lit by the sinking sun that's burning like a giant golden flare under clear water.

Her Daddy, Gyr says, died two weeks ago of a heart attack. He was a non-stop talker, an adrenaline junky, a welder with a face pitted from sparks. He rode a motorcycle—often into things, fast. In the Absorakas, following a grizzly sow too closely, he was mauled. The bear's mouth gaped over his head but for some reason didn't bite down, though he carried tooth scars on his forehead. The pain from all his wounds was so severe that he took methadone, which dissolved his short-term memory. In the past couple of years, he had to write down everything on scraps of paper.

A cool breeze blows.

"He loved his pets," she says. "They were his best friends. He treated me like a princess. And he was fascinated with animals. Even went to UW for a semester to be a biologist, but he was too busy hunting, massacring prairie dogs for fun."

Flynn thinks he hears a whistle blowing in the distance, maybe even smells Danny's cheesecake on the wind. Hunger tugs at his stomach. A colorful sky spreads mural-like across the western horizon. A coyote, in silhouette, prances over the rocky landscape.

"What's it like to be a coyote prowling near timberline on a fall evening?" Gyr whispers. "Does it enjoy the gentle night, the colorful sky? Is it anxious about the coming winter? Does it mourn fallen family members? Does some scent on the wind carry a memory? Or is hunger its only companion?"

Flynn wants to enter into the obscure world of the beast, but try as he might, he can't get outside his circumscribed thoughts. He is merely Tommy Flynn, a greedy, horny, unimaginative young man. He turns to Gyr, her eyes a brown fire of concentration. She seems to slip into places where he can't follow. Envy stirs inside him, followed by that hot burst of desire. He thinks, *She is as wild and wanton as a weasel.* He puts his hand on her nylon pants and rubs softly. His hand climbs up her leg, past her knee, up the taught flesh of hamstring, until he feels a stabbing pain on the back of his hand.

"Shit," he cries. "That hurt like hell!"

Gyr pulls a red Swiss Army knife away from his hand, the corkscrew out like a scorpion's tail. "You're lucky I didn't jab the knife blade into your hand."

"How about just telling me to stop?"

"This way you get the message. No misunderstandings."

She marches down the mountain, disappearing into the dusk. His hand trickles blood from a jagged hole. He wraps a bandanna around it and heads back to camp. It is near dark when he returns, and Aaron is waiting, fingering his whistle. He thinks Aaron might blow it right now, giving him a technical, or kicking him out of the game altogether.

"Damn Flynn," Aaron says, his voice shrill. "What the hell? We didn't know if you'd fallen off a cliff or what?"

Flynn holds his hand out to Aaron, who shines a flashlight on the wound. "What happened?"

Aaron goes to his tent and returns with a first-aid kit and cleans out the wound with water and iodine. As he wraps Flynn's hand in gauze and a cloth bandage, the others come around and talk, giving him a plate of cheesecake and a cup of hot cocoa. They all have stories of foolish people—sometimes themselves, in their younger years—who have wandered off the path and gotten into trouble: poison ivy, bee stings, strained knees, hypothermia, etc. The body heat and the food warms Flynn as the cold stars shine in the clear sky.

Flynn lies awake, his hand pulsing with rejection. A patina of hoarfrost, lit up by a quarter moon, coats the rocks and grasses. Cold air seeps into his open tent and down his sleeping bag as he tries to unravel the mystery of Gyr. Her father, her Daddy, has fucked her up good. She mourns the eccentric coot, even as she puzzles out his incongruities: animal lover and bloodthirsty hunter, devoted father and screwball. He has attempted to work out similar inconsistencies in his own father's life: how his father could be such a solid citizen, well-respected in the community, faithful to his wife even after her death, and yet could go into an upscale bar and laugh at the ugliest jokes—what's the difference between a 16-inch pizza and a thirty-year-old black man? The pizza can feed a family of four. What do you say to a woman with two black eyes? Nothing. She's already been told twice.

Father's, he concludes, are our first guides: they trail blaze a certain direction, but they don't know what they are doing any more than we do. At some point, we must strike off on our own equally foolish paths.

The next day they hike hard for ten miles while a storm batters them. The sky roils over the mountains like cement being mixed. Cold rain lashes at them in the open country. Coats, ponchos, and pack covers snap about bodies and faces in the wind. The group struggles forward, joking at first, then grumbling, then complaining bitterly to Aaron and Danny, saying, in essence, *What idiot would plan a trip into the mountains in September?*

"The bugs aren't bad," Aaron shouts. "The trail isn't crowded. You shouldn't have to use much sunscreen."

"No-one is going to get heat stroke," Danny chimes in. "At least we aren't dead."

"Not yet," the others grimly answer.

At mid-day, they head down from the pass into the narrow confines of Upper Cascade Canyon, between granite cliffs and beside a roaring stream, coming into a conifer forest. They reach camp in two more hours, and Aaron and Danny string up a tarp to cook under as the others put up their tents. At supper, the talk is all about getting off the trail, heading into town for a big meal, checking emails, calling home and work.

In the cold morning, they eat breakfast, break camp, and hurtle down the trail to Lower Cascade Canyon. In a couple of miles, they reach a trail junction, which offers two choices: the right leads down to roads and restaurants, the left heads up to Lake Solitude.

Flynn taps Aaron on the shoulder. "I'm going to follow this trail for a while and camp at the lake."

"Are you sure?" Aaron asks.

Flynn nods. Danny offers Flynn some left over food: a hunk of cheddar cheese, two sleeves of broken Ritz crackers, a Power Bar. The others tempt him with suggestions of warm hotel beds and clean linens, hot showers and meals, Italian wines. Aaron makes him sign a note that he has voluntarily left the group. He waves and heads off on his own.

Climbing, searching the melting snow for signs, all he sees are a few elk tracks. In the early evening, he reaches the round, green lake, tucked into a basin surrounded on three sides by mountains. Except for on the highest peaks, the snow has melted. The lake is in shadow. He has eaten the rest of his food and his stomach growls. He lays his sleeping bag out on a tarp and falls asleep.

He wakes to a cold blue morning and spends an hour watching ducks bobbing on the sparkling green water, so hungry he ponders catching one and eating it raw. His mind releases an obscure memory: a summer evening playing hide and seek, climbing a maple tree and coming face to face with a robin sitting on its nest. Neither of them moved for fifteen minutes. When the bird finally flew, he felt himself flying away too, rising out of the nest, all hollow bones and feathers, darting through that green, leafy world out into the open.

At supper, excited, he told his father about it, but his father just grunted once and kept eating and reading invoices.

He spots Gyr coming down from a rocky route above the lake, wearing a white T-shirt, hiking pants, and her pack. She looks tiny, maybe under a hundred pounds. She heads to the shoreline next to Flynn, takes off her pack, and sits cross-legged, polishing an apple. She stares at him, as though she is studying a bug. "You're an interesting specimen, Flynn."

"Why?"

"There might be some promise to you. You might amount to something yet. You might not be a total loss."

"I was Petoskey's young executive of the year last year."

"Even so."

"Thanks," he says. He raises his injured hand, swaddled in bandages, and she shrugs, gives him a *what the hell did you expect* look.

"I came here to remember my Daddy. You were feeling me up at the funeral."

Flynn picks a blade of grass and throws it into the breeze. He sits with his legs crossed, disciple-like, waiting for Gyr to speak. His stomach growls so loudly she hands him an apple and some cheese.

She looks out over the lake. "He taught me a lot. About the mountains, but mostly about animals. He showed me how to track them, to capture and hunt them, to kill them. But I don't think that's for me."

Her eyes are glistening, as though someone has put on too much shellac, her lower lip trembling slightly.

"I try to learn everything I can about an animal. How are their eyes different from ours? Can they see colors, ultraviolet light? Can they hear things beyond our ability, like a dog whistle? An elephant can hear sounds as low as 5 hertz, while we can't hear anything lower than 20 hertz. A porpoise can hear sounds up to 450,000 hertz, way beyond our limit."

"Reality," says Flynn, "is the aggregate of the senses of all creatures."

Gyr stares at him, mouth open.

"I read it somewhere," he says, shrugging. "On a calendar, I think."

Gyr flashes a crooked smile. "What must it be like to smell something five miles away? To live for only two summers? All of those things. I want to enter into their worlds, to experience their desires, their fears... How can I kill something that can feel all that?"

They spend the afternoon at Lake Solitude talking about animals, about fathers, and eating apples and cheese. As the sun sinks below the peaks, they begin the long climb to the pass at the divide. Near the top, the evening sky fading into a watery blue, a large bird flies towards them, soaring above the valley.

They stop.

Gyr places her hands on his chest.

"You are flying," she whispers hypnotically, "over a valley in the mountains, heading to your aerie."

In the thin air he relaxes, tries to become as receptive as the boy in the maple tree, and his body lightens. He is airborne, heading to his mountainside ledge in the next valley. His stomach is full of snake and warm. The world is paler, sepia-toned, though he has never seen with such acuity before. The swimmers in his vision are gone. He spies movement in the rocks below—a pika scurrying for cover, a marmot peering out from its rocky lair. Air rushes over his outstretched wings. A collar of feathers rustles about his neck. Transparent eyelids wipe the dust away from his eyes.

"You have two foveae in your retinas," Gyr says, "so you have two focal points—one ahead of you, and one to the side. A nictitating membrane."

He focuses on the moment, on each slow-motion wing beat. He knows nothing of the past or the future, nothing of regret or vanity or worry, nothing of choice. Two hominids look up at him, but they are of no interest. He crosses over into the next valley, sees the body of blue water his aerie looks over. Before he heads to his shelter for the night, with a few powerful wing beats, he soars higher, up into the sky toward the first stars, for the sheer joy of it.

Seventy-Eight

Bethany Reid

The clearcut devastates the ridge,
ground scarred with ragged stumps,
brush stacked and burned.
Almost hidden, seedlings of Douglas fir
poke up green heads
and my father points them out with the toe
of his boot. *This one will make it,*
this one. Not this one. The top, he explains,
has been nibbled away by deer.
He stoops to tug it from the ground.
The year he moved here, he tells me,
the year of my birth, the timber company
poisoned the deer
and though they quickly rebounded,
for ten years anything that fed from the carcasses
disappeared. Coyote and vulture and bear,
red tailed hawk, eagle. *Well, the coyotes*
came back fast enough. Dad steps
onto a stump. It's like a platform, that big,
and I climb up beside him, as he counts
the rings. *One, two, three...*
then by fives, and finishing, *seventy-eight,*

his age. It's a shame
to have cut it down I tell him
and he scoffs. *Seventy-eight is a lot of years.*
What do we love in this world?
What do we destroy? Why are these
so often the same things?
I kneel to trace for myself
the concentric rings down to the heartwood.

Innocence

It is August, 1999, and my baby daughter
is one month old. The family gathers,

even the oldest of my aunts still hale enough
to hold a baby. After the blessing,
my sister and I remain, spending a few days

in our childhood home along with our older children,
their shouts wafting through open doors

like news from far away, echoes across water.

The baby fusses, and when my oldest nephew
lies down on the couch, my sister
puts the baby on his chest. They both fall asleep.

In September my nephew will join the Marines.
My sister and I sit watching, talking softly

about everything and nothing. What will happen

has not yet happened. We bask
in the enormous safety of the afternoon.

Fallow, And Falling Behind

Paula Marafino Bernett

The field lies fallow,
Gathering its wits about it.
One of the mourners,
Trudging by the upheaved clods
And little risen dusts
Is falling behind the cortege.
She is gathering her griefs
Into her, resting the worn-out
Grounds, leaving unseeded
The exhausted fields of her life.
For now, the wind, the beating sun,
And the turning of the worms
Is enough.

In the Absence of Beauty

Gina Troisi

As a child, I knew him in a heart-colored house in a quaint green neighborhood in Massachusetts. In a ranch house with white shutters and perfectly manicured hedges that lined the neat, square patch of front lawn. I played waitress there using clear glass ashtrays, some of which I left empty, while filling others with egg-shaped gelatin candies. They were sugar covered, as if sprinkled with shards of crystals. I placed them on coffee tables, in front of imaginary people sitting on the loveseat, and on end tables. I created stacks of clutter, stashing them in corners of the house like small jewels.

My grandfather, Nanu received the empty ashtrays with delight. "Thank you GG! This is delicious," he said, opening his mouth wide to accept invisible salads and chicken soup, scooping them up with imaginary forks and spoons.

My Nana, Regina, lived there with him. She sat with crossed legs, her fingers long and extended, holding cigarettes in between the first and second, the paper around them staining her flesh yellow. She offered me patchwork ice cream topped with Vienna Fingers, which I eagerly accepted. Together, we watched black and white murder mysteries on television, and I fell in love with Perry Mason. She'd let me sit in Nanu's recliner, and I'd tuck myself into the large leather seat wearing her rosaries around my neck. The onyx beads used to busy me for hours, as I recited Hail Marys and Our Fathers. When Nanu finished painting in the basement, he'd come upstairs to listen to me sounding the prayers, and smile. "Did your grandmother teach you that?" When I was done, he'd tickle me until I fell out of the chair—until I was exhausted from laughter.

My Nanu glanced in his wife's direction with love, his mouth curved in a half joking grin. "What do you think, Reggie?" He'd playfully poke her in the ribs while stirring homemade tomato sauce, flinging a dishtowel over his shoulder. It would land clumsily across his neck, and she'd smile. He always hugged her for lengths of time.

I stayed overnight at my grandparents' house when my mother needed a break from tending to three young children, which was often. My two older sisters, Krista and Lisa, usually stayed home since they were already in school. At bedtime, I molded myself into my grandfather's bed wearing his worn yellow t-shirts that hung just below my knees. He'd pinch my cheek while I said my prayers and say, "Ciao Bella." When I was done, I'd curl up next to him with my head on his strong shoulder, and fall into deep sleep.

When my sister, Krista, telephoned about Nanu's hospital admission, I was twenty-three years old. He was eighty-two. He had woken from sleep, gasping for air. Alone in the dark bedroom, he reached for the nightstand. He dialed 911 with his half crippled fingers, trying to squeeze sensation into them like a person dangling from a ledge.

When she called to tell me this, I was kneeling in a borrowed bedroom in New Hampshire, stuffing a yellow t-shirt into my duffel bag, in the midst of packing my Chevy to drive down to Florida, where he lived. The past few weeks he'd been preparing for my arrival—filling the cupboards with Rice Krispies and gallons of Charlotte Russe wine, and stocking the freezer with homemade lasagna.

I was not only going to Florida to visit Nanu; I was on my way to Panama City Beach to live and apprentice with Ursula, my herbalist friend. Ursula aided me when I detoxified from drugs a few years before, prescribing roots and tinctures, loading me up with capsules and herbs. When I quit drugs, I replaced them with bottles of wine and spiked coffee in the mornings—not because I needed to, but more out of boredom—and for some time, I'd known I needed to leave. I needed a hiatus. It felt right that I was leaving then, after college, to start a new life.

On the phone, Krista said, "They think it's his gallbladder, but they've admitted him because they want to do some tests. They've ruled out all forms of cancer, so it shouldn't be too much to worry about."

But why would his gallbladder make him lose his breath? And why hadn't he called a neighbor to take him to the hospital? I couldn't imagine how alone he had been, how afraid.

For a man who wore an ace bandage after falling off his bike, but lied to us and said, "This? This is an old football injury," I knew that if it wasn't for the loss of breath, he'd be trying to mend himself at home under his own supervision. Nanu had never been admitted to the hospital before.

When I called room twenty-four, a hoarse voice answered. It sounded like his vocal cords were shredded, like uttering a simple word was unbearable. "Hi, Nanu."

"Hi, GG."

"I'm leaving to come down tomorrow," I said.

"GG, it really isn't a good time, I won't be at the house. I'm very sick."

"I still think I should come. I'll clean up and I can come stay with you at the hospital until you're back on your feet. Besides, who's going to eat all that food?"

"No, it really isn't a good time, GG." I could barely make out his slow, scarce words. *Who was this person on the other end of the phone with laryngitis? How was he so sick, when he'd been fine? When was the last time I'd heard from him?*

I felt bad keeping him on the line—it sounded like hot tea was scorching his throat, as if he was trying to utter words in between scaldings. I said, "Okay, I love you. Talk to you soon."

But I was still going to Florida. I was not going to let the man I loved most in the world be alone in a hospital, listening to vague test results from disorganized doctors.

The driving was meditative. Although my internal voice had always been busier than its external twin, the drive helped it to relax; spans of time allowed it to forget its restlessness—its uneasiness. I thought about what Nanu and I might do for the next few weeks, after he recovered. Maybe we'd go for a hike by the coast, me insisting that he hand over the lawn chairs, and him refusing to let me carry them. Maybe I'd sit on the screened-in porch and edit some old poems while he painted, duplicating a nature magazine photo or a graphic he'd printed off of the computer. Or maybe a harbor cruise would suit us, one where we could gamble, like we'd been doing more and more since he'd grown too tired to take care of his own boat.

By the time I reached the Smoky Mountains of North Carolina, I felt worlds apart from the life I had been leading—I had just said good-bye to a new lover. It was the type of affair one must leave just as it begins, mostly because that's what it constituted—an affair, and also because I'd been avoiding asking about the drug problem I knew he had. I had been obsessed for weeks, even months—obsessed with his hair's waves, the freckles on his shoulders, and the surface of his skin. I had been obsessed to the point of distraction at the restaurant where we worked, fumbling up orders, bringing customers wrong meals, and spilling drinks at tables. My obsession had been boiling over into other parts of my life, like when the phone rang, and I hoped it was him, and when it wasn't I still heard his voice in my head while trying to have a conversation with someone else. Like a new and exciting career, this affair had been all-consuming. Like a narcotic, it had numbed me for a while.

I cruised around the curves, weaving in and out of the mountains. The trees stood bold against the charcoal mist. The fog stilled the air around the red and silver maples. I wondered about my Nanu's older sister, Christina, who lived somewhere around these woods. How he'd say, "My sister lives there," with even the slightest mention of the Smokies. "Simply beautiful." As my teal Chevy S10 pick up meandered around the rolling hills, climbing up and gliding down, I heard CDs and backpacks and books roll around in the cab of the truck. More trees—striped maples and mountain maples. The cell phone on the passenger seat rang, sounding like tambourines. It took me by surprise, since I'd borrowed it from a friend for emergency purposes. I picked it up.

"You'd better just turn around." Krista's voice was feverish, her sobs loud and unruly.

"What?" I lowered Paul Simon's "Graceland" with my other hand.

She tried to steady her voice. "Nanu's dying," she said, finding breaths in between her words. "They gave him two weeks to live. It's cancer of the esophagus."

What was she talking about? This was absurd, unbelievable, and definitely some sort of mistake. "Whoa, slow down Krissy, what are you talking about?"

"The doctors are saying he has one of the worst cases of esophageal cancer that they've ever seen. He must have been sick for a while and kept it a secret... you'd better just turn around. Dad is flying him up to New Hampshire to die..." A secret? What was this? How could Nanu have known? He couldn't have—he must have believed it was his gallbladder. *I won't be at home GG. I'm very sick.*

I couldn't hear her anymore. Tones rang in my ears, creeping up each side of my head. I remembered Nanu talking about having to eat foods with less flavoring the last couple of months because of heartburn; it had seemed normal for an eighty-two year old who'd been eating tomato sauce and drinking red wine his entire life. That was the only thing that had been out of the ordinary, besides the less frequent phone calls, but were they even less frequent? With my recent infatuation and my move, I'd been neglecting our Sunday phone calls, which I usually depended on.

I saw opaque clouds through the rearview mirror. It was twilight, and carnation pink hid behind blue gray. The clouds stretched across the sky, wedging in between layers of the universe, he and I falling like microscopic drops of ink on the earth's canvas. Fading.

I thought back to our last annual visit to Florida. It was on Thanksgiving, which was also my birthday. Nanu was equipped with a bottle of sparkling Korbel Brut, so we toasted champagne, clinking our glasses together in celebration of the new year ahead. He'd told all his friends in the old folks' park, "My granddaughters are coming to visit. One of them is a rebel (Krista), and the other one's a hippie (me). He and I debated herbal medicines and shared thoughts on Christianity.

Although Nanu spent his life working with his hands as the owner of his own plumbing company, he was an avid reader and we regularly discussed his findings, from prostate health to the origin of the world, from Adam and Eve to Darwin, from Nazi Germany to Bin Laden. As usual, he told me to relax, to ease up on my perpetual paranoia, my concerns about toxic tap water, and to live more like him, without worries. A wonderful idea, but impossible for me. Krista and I joked with him about it over salad with blue cheese crumbs, homemade sautéed greens, and pizza dough.

Nanu was wide-minded for an old man. He supported my participation in pro-abortion rallies in Washington D.C. "I believe women should make the choice when it comes to their own bodies." He encouraged road trips across the country, and my desire to take time off to think long and hard about whether or not I wanted to go to college. "Just another experience. I think that's wonderful, GG," he'd say in response to my idea to drive further, to see more ground, when friends and family members insisted my notions were poorly thought out and unrealistic—that I'd never go to college if I didn't go right away, and that I was wasting time working in restaurants. "Maybe you'll be like Nancy, and become a manager," Nanu said about my boss, whom I admired.

After hanging up with Krista, I dialed the hospital again. I wanted to tell Nanu that the Smokies were every bit as beautiful as he'd described, so I did. "There are wildflowers everywhere. I think they've just bloomed. And I drove by a waterfall in just the right light. It's like a little paradise."

"Okay, GG. I'm glad you're there."

"I'll see you soon. I'm on my way back home. I love you," I said.

I stopped at a campground in Ashville and set up my tent by a wind-ing river. Taking my time to gather branches, I started a small fire. I smoked cigarettes while drinking a large Heineken by the light of the flames, and cried. My body carried far too much weight. It felt strapped to the ground, as if in a straightjacket. I played solitaire for a while, and tried to feed myself spoonfuls of peanut butter, but it was useless. No hunger visited, not the physical kind. The rushing river soared through the trees, ripping through mossy branches—I lost my-self to the sound. For moments, I heard nothing else, not even my own thoughts.

It was late, but I couldn't sleep, so I stayed sitting on the dirt watching logs form bridges across the water. Sitting with the birches in the mountains by the river, I wondered if Nanu was lying awake in the hospital on an uncomfortable bed, in a room with white walls—I thought about how he was at peace in the woods, how he needed to see this place where I sat and to feel its magic, even though I could not.

Scraping my sneakers against the dirt I made shapes, thinking about how my life had intersected his, how our piles of memories were made up over time, how the absence of my father, his son, had deep-ened our union, had fed it and fueled it. I thought about how even though he'd served in the Navy, he never talked about the war, how no one did. Instead, he talked of Hawaii, of Japan, of his travels during that time. I remembered his strength when dealing with his younger son and my father's brother, Dicky, who battled with heroin for twenty years before dying—how Nanu used his savings to send him to rehabs, to bail him out of jail, and then how he pretended not to be crushed when it turned out to be for nothing. I thought about my lover, an ad-dict—someone's father and someone else's son, and how I wanted him near me now. Sitting, I cradled my knees until the sun rose.

When day broke, I crawled back into the tent to nap. I finally fell asleep, but Nanu visited my dreams, stumbling over words he couldn't pronounce. He was trying to talk to me, to tell me something. Attempting to respond, I'd open my mouth, but each time I discovered I lost my voice. In sleep, my vocal cords severed, and my lungs lost their breath. In sleep, panic barged in.

My father, who I called Jim, was going to be flying Nanu up to New Hampshire. I hadn't talked to him in years. I'd been angry with him since I could remember, since he'd left us when I was six. He left us because he was having multiple affairs, the most significant one with his secretary, Brenda, who he married months after divorcing my mother. Brenda discouraged him from spending time with my sisters and me, and he obliged. She threatened us during screaming matches, saying she wouldn't allow us to ruin her marriage, a marriage which she'd worked long and hard for during the years when my parents were together.

Jim used his defense attorney skills to interrogate my sisters and me our entire lives, as if we were the prosecutors, as if we were always on the opposite side. He followed Brenda's wishes and demands until she finally divorced him after nine years of marriage, and then he tried to reconcile with us, not as a father, but as a friend who wanted us to understand his misery. He wanted to tell us about how she'd wronged him; he wanted us to feel his pain. By that point, I was well into high school, and still trying to deal with my own pain, so I told him I had surpassed the need for a father.

Nanu was being taken to Jim's gigantic house on the lake, despite the fact that he never wanted to leave Florida, where he took pride in golfing, boating, and painting. He was being taken to a house filled with a family I'd never met, and a woman, Deb, I'd seen only once from afar—who had long Barbie-like hair, a slender figure, and a straight, pointed, witch-like nose. What would my sisters and I do there, seeing Nanu for his last days and breaths?

My life seemed to stretch along the highway like a path I'd keep following until it dropped off the earth. I was moving to Florida, but Nanu wouldn't be there any longer. I wanted to pour him a glass of wine and wake him up from this staggering sickness. Outside, the moon was almost full. Shimmers of silver flashed across the windshield. I saw his golden brown eyes. I saw the ambulance. And surges of red. Red, streaking like lightning.

I pushed north on 95. I drove from state to state for sixteen hours, stopping only to use bathrooms and buy cappuccinos from sticky convenience store machines. I drove until I reached my mother's house in New Hampshire, until my eyes were red and swollen, until my neck was stiff with exhaustion. When I arrived, it was late at night, and I collapsed in the guest bedroom, sleeping soundly through the entire next day.

Deb, Krista, and I stood nervously at the gate inside the airport. Deb's profile reminded me of Brenda's, the sharp cheek bone structure and the triangular nose. Her clothes were looser—she wore a long linen dress that belled out just underneath her small breasts— like a maternity dress. Brenda usually wore denim, too tight across her wide bottom, and shirts that dipped down between her small, pear-shaped breasts. The blonde woman was fair, with sky-blue eyes and only a touch of makeup. "Are you girls close with him?" Deb asked.

"Yes." I couldn't speak any further. I scanned the people, trying to halt my whirling thoughts. *How did he handle this torturous plane ride? Did he even want to be here? Was he scared?* I was terrified.

There was Jim. He looked aged, wrinkled, and unattractive, as if his face was losing its symmetry. He pushed a wheelchair, too quickly it seemed, his feet fumbling beneath him, lost. In the chair sat an old man that I didn't recognize. He was skinny, almost emaciated, his face sunken in so deep that his brown eyes almost popped out of his head. His clothes were hanging from the wheel chair, barely fitting him. He looked restless, his fingers shaking like he'd just suffered electric shock therapy. His hands didn't look like his. I knew them as thick and darkened by sun, with strong tendons from years of working as a plumber. His hands were small now, the fingers shriveled and dry and old, so old. His hands didn't belong to him. On his face, he wore an expression between pain and fear, as if he was in too much pain to be scared, and too scared to feel the pain. If I didn't know this was my Nanu, I might have thought he was a concentration camp victim who'd just been released, but had no hope of surviving. I couldn't hide my shock; I'd never seen death this close.

He didn't say hello and neither did we. We were still like trees on a windless day.

"I have to pee," he said.

"Okay, okay," Jim responded. They'd done this before. "He has to pee," Jim said, with a quick glance over at us. We nodded, our bodies motionless, soundless. Jim wheeled Nanu around the corner into the restroom. His motions were automatic, but his face looked flustered and his breath sounded winded. I couldn't imagine him assisting Nanu in a bathroom stall—a man who had three children, but had probably never changed a diaper or fed an infant a bottle, ever.

Krista looked over at me. "Oh my God," she said, her mouth wide open.

On the way back from the airport, the car filled with flustered small talk, mostly from Jim, which I could barely hear. Krista stared blankly at the highway, while I sank back into the slippery leather seat and rested my head against the window. He mentioned that hospice people were coming to the house. There was conversation about a bed in a room. *A death bed?* Jim was matter-of-fact, stating what we needed to know. I was looking at Nanu in the passenger side mirror while Jim talked as if he wasn't even there, as if he were already gone. *This is what will happen. We won't ask you, because you have lost your voice.* I wanted to talk to him, but I had no words, and I imagined that it was painful for him to talk. His pupils were dilated from the morphine running through veins and arteries. I'd never seen his eyes this wide open; they looked so large that I believed all he could see was death.

The road to Jim's house wound itself along the edges of a lake. It was a dirt road, like one you might take to a summer camp or cottage. The house was beige, with a balcony overlooking the lake, just before a cul-de-sac. The driveway was a horseshoe, with a garage underneath the balcony. I wondered who lived there. I knew Deb had daughters, but I didn't know if they were grown or not, and I didn't ask. I didn't want Nanu to worry that Krista and I were as uncomfortable as he might have been about spending our last days together in this house.

Jim, Krista, and I crouched around the wheelchair and lifted it up the front stairs and into the house. Each wheel had its own struggle; we had to turn the chair and tip it just so, without moving him too much. I didn't expect this—that he'd be unable to walk or move. Nanu was wordless, but I knew he was also sickened. We were doing our best to keep it still, but we were clumsy with the chair, and I suspected that each shake was painful. When I didn't think it was possible for his eyes to grow wider, they did, this time with shame.

Once inside, Jim wheeled Nanu into the bathroom again. Krista and I stood in the living room for a second. "Make yourselves at home, girls," Deb said. "Here, I'll take your bags." A baby grand piano sat in the corner, in front of the staircase, and I wondered if she played because Jim didn't. The kitchen and living room connected, forming one room. The wallpaper was peach with white petunias, and black and white Ansel Adams prints ornamented the walls. Snow covered pines. A rose and driftwood. Yosemite in the summertime. The balcony was off of this room, with immaculate windows lining the front of the house. The sun glowed over the water, amplifying the vast lake view.

Deb dropped our bags in the master bedroom, where she had prepared a hospital-type bed. It was for Nanu to lie on—for him to die on. The bed was white, crisp, and sterile. There was nothing gentle or kind about it, like fluffy satin throw pillows or fleece blankets. The pillowcases looked icy and their crinkled edges drooped over the sides. *They're too big*, I thought. Nanu and Jim were still in the bathroom, and Deb motioned to Krista and me. She pointed to a small gold crucifix in between her thumb and pointer finger. "I'm sneaking this under his pillow," she whispered. I didn't understand why she was telling us this. I didn't know what approval she sought. She placed it between the sandpaper pillowcase and the fold-up cot. I glared at her from across the room, battling my lips to stay closed, to drown her out. We all knew that Nanu wasn't Christian, or even slightly religious. *Who was she trying to console?*

Bach's *Brandenburg Concerto* played on the stereo in the bedroom. Krista and I made ourselves as comfortable as possible, sitting on the edge of the bed that was nearest him. Deb called from the kitchen, offering us pizza, but we refused. I couldn't eat. Nanu wouldn't take water or food; how could I? This was a man whose mantra had been, "Eating and drinking are two of the finest things in life."

Nanu closed his eyes and Krista and I reclined on the flowery bedspread. Jim and Deb busied themselves out in the living room; they were making plans for urns and ashes and undertakers. They'd told us we were welcome to "camp out" here for a couple of weeks. When I told my mother that I was going to bring my tent and set it up in the yard, she said, "No, Gina. I think they meant to 'sleep over,' not to bring your tent."

I watched the grooves in the ceiling. I tried to meditate on them while Nanu drifted off, but I only saw him grow sicker and sicker, swirling down into a pool of I didn't know what. Blackness. I missed him and he wasn't even gone. I missed him painting furiously to the very music we listened to, shaping a white seagull with its wings spread, shades of aqua marine water rippling across the canvas. Exquisite. I missed the two of us at sunset in Florida, at the dock by the canal. I recalled one of our last times there, when I was mesmerized by the sunset, its orange, glowing glare. "Don't ever look directly at the sun before it descends, GG."

"Really? I always do. I'm too impatient."

"No, you shouldn't. It's not good for your retinas." His face was serious, as if he'd use all the power in him to protect my eyes—my eyes that saw him as strong and able, not breaking as he was now. Not broken. I was twenty-two, but we held hands as if I were still three years old, as if he needed to be sure that I wouldn't go blind, that I wouldn't lose my vision. My bare feet squished into the damp mud. At the dock, we had nothing to say. Our silence spoke and followed us here to this awful beige bedroom in New Hampshire.

Nanu lay on the white twin bed, his eyes half open, while Krista and I listened to Jim and Deb bustle around the kitchen. They talked about food, and about setting up a bedroom for themselves upstairs. They were taking care of laundry and paperwork and phone calls— taking care of the things that go along with death. Death, hanging in the air like a dark storm cloud waiting to break.

A bucket rested on the bureau. In between bouts of sleep, Nanu propped his head up, bile forcing itself up his esophagus. When we heard him begin to clear his throat, Krista and I jumped. I propped his shoulders up while she held the bucket. His shoulders were sharp and pointed, like blades. Our touches pained him, but if we didn't lift him, he'd choke.

Listening to Bach reminded me of landing in Fort Myers and plopping myself into his white Crown Victoria, the classical music blaring. Of how he'd look at me. "Isn't this beautiful, GG?"

"Yes," I'd say, and turn ahead to take in the palm trees. I'd open my window all the way, and soak in the warmth of just having gotten off the plane.

But we weren't there any longer. We were here, in the absence of beauty.

During the waiting, Lisa walked in, tanned from the Arizona sun. She wore corduroy overalls and a tie-dyed tank top. She leaned down and kissed our grandfather on the cheek. "Hi Nanu."

"Hi Lis." He forced the words out of his mouth, each syllable scraping the back of his throat.

"Can I read to you from the Bible?" Lisa, a born again Christian, went nowhere without her righteous book. Nanu, whose father became a Jehovah's Witness during his childhood, was an atheist. After his mother died from a brain tumor in her late twenties, his father began bringing the New Testament to the dinner table each night. His father would holler, pound his fists, and insist that his children believe in paradise. He'd demand that they believe in being chosen. "Why do you think I was dying to join the Navy?" Nanu said often. After leaving home, he rejected organized religion, believing that once a person died, he or she lay in the ground for all eternity. We'd discussed this many times before.

"Sure, Lis." Lisa began to read, while Krista and I looked at each other. Lisa had lived out west for years so we didn't see her often, and each time we did she arrived with a new idea about how she'd been rebirthed, or cleaned her slate. The last time, after years of sexual relations, she came back east a virgin.

We knew that Nanu wouldn't have us sit by him for days while he fragmented. Water glazed his pupils. They had stars in the center. Glistening stars. I imagined that he was petrified—his face a picture of the way young children and the elderly mesh, the way we become like children again as we age, scared of first steps and new colors, insecure about what life brings us next. Or where it will deliver us. I felt his fear the way I felt a cat's pain after it was hit by a car—some people can leave a scene like that unaffected, but I couldn't desensitize myself. Death to me was like a million blades riding against my spine, inching their way into each vertebra to penetrate my skull. My temples pulsed. My limbs felt weak again. Cramps rode up my calves and I felt trapped, as he must have, as if I were about to fall over into a pit of eternal flames. I wanted to stand up for Nanu against the enormous God in the sky.

I thought back to the day when I was about to speak in a Catholic church, at my grandmother's funeral, but my tears poured and my voice shook with stutters. The priest turned to me with an impatient face and said, "Well, if you can't do this...."

My Nanu, standing next to me, looked directly into the face of the man with the white collar. "Hey, this is an empowered woman you're talking to." The priest didn't respond. I was twenty years old then. Nanu's gift to me was grace.

Out in the kitchen, there was more mention of hospice. In the bedroom, we pretended not to listen, not to hear. A priest. The name of a nurse. Tomorrow she'd be here, or the next day. I couldn't even imagine a tomorrow when today was filled with yelps and shivers and alkaline fluid. When today silence wrapped itself around us like a torn blanket in the cold winter. Nanu was uncomfortable, but he couldn't move. He was unable to leave, unlike me, prone to bolt at the slightest sight of trouble.

I turned up the knob on the Panasonic boom box, and Chopin's notes ascended and then fell, settling somewhere between a storm and an idle day—containing vast differences, like a plane lifting serenely into the sky, and then its crashing explosion. Lisa raised her reading voice: "The Lord is my strength and my shield...."

Jim and Deb entered the bedroom. Deb reminded us to help ourselves to the fridge while we were there. She looked like she felt sorry for Krista and I; we were crying, still on the bed. Lisa still sat in a chair by Nanu's bed reading aloud, her legs stretched out, sustained by the footrest. Nanu closed his eyes again. He'd been doing this for hours—opening his eyes, then closing them, then the bile. His loss of voice shocked me the most—the reality that the day I found out about

the cancer our conversations ceased—as if years worth of disease sud-
denly shattered our communication. But it hadn't; he had already been
invaded, for who knows how long.

Jim didn't know we'd heard their conversations. "Hey," he said,
and Lisa stopped reading. "The hospice nurse will come over tomor-
row, or the next day. She won't sleep here, but she'll help out most
hours of the day." I hated that Nanu was like a mannequin in the
room, that no one talked to him, but only around him. I hated that I
couldn't talk with him, but I had no words that mattered anyway.

My sisters and I nodded at Jim.

Nanu jerked his head up. His head that had not moved for
hours. "This is not going to be prolonged." The voice was loud despite
its sparseness, his declaration so strong that Lisa dropped the book.
She sat by his bedside, its pages flung open. "Did you hear me?" He
was looking at Jim—warning Jim, and comforting us. I broke. Krista
broke. Even Lisa broke. I felt like I was five years old; I sensed aban-
donment, like a small child dropped off at the mall alone, her parents
taking off down the road. I broke.

He looked at me, helpless, as if to say, *What do you want me
to do, GG?* His pain was fierce, disease violently eating bits of his
esophagus. His caved in features showed distress, his skin tightening.
How could this be happening? We still had more to talk about. I still
needed his wisdom. Here I was, after bringing myself back from drugs
and destruction, still plunging into pain, still in love with danger. Here
I was, hoping that Ursula would cleanse and purify me—hoping that
by moving, I'd be absolved.

The morphine drove his eyes mad, the stars dancing as the
chamber music perpetuated in the background. With each moment in
between, when he closed his eyes, I thought he'd surrender to death.

But he continued to open them, wide now, his pupils enlarged. This couldn't possibly go on for days, my sisters and me without words in this crowded bedroom. Jim, trying to get Nanu to take some dribbles of water, or some ice cubes, which he continuously refused. didn't want to let go of his father, and for moments, I didn't blame him.

It was two o'clock in the morning when Nanu mentioned the Virgin. It happened just after Krista looked at Deb and Jim, sitting in chairs against the wall, and said, "You two should go to bed. Get some sleep. We can stay up with him."

"Okay," Jim said. "We'll be right upstairs. But I'll give him his pill first." He struggled with Nanu, who didn't want to swallow, who didn't want to be touched. Jim crushed the pill with his fingers, and fed bits of it in between Nanu's lips. "To kill the pain," Jim said. "Really, just take it." It was difficult to tell whether Nanu had swallowed it or not, but at least it was inside his mouth now. "Good night, Dad. Good night, girls." They left.

Nanu closed his eyes. "She's walking through the village."

"Who?" I asked.

"Mary. The Virgin. She's walking in between the rows of people."

Krista, Lisa, and I looked at one another. "She's there," he said, his eyes closed. I tried to imagine brick walls where the Virgin walked; I tried to imagine what he saw. I wondered what verses Lisa had been reading to him; I hadn't listened, not to the meaning of the words. I thought of Jerusalem, dirt roads and temples and cloaks.

Later, Lisa said she thought he was talking to Jesus. Later, I said he hallucinated from the morphine. Later, Krista forgot what he said.

He leaned toward us then, curving his head slightly to the left, toward my side of the bed. With enormous black eyes, he looked at me and winked. Just like that. No one said a word.

I gaped at him. His eyes were suspended, inviting me into their emptiness. I didn't see the village or the Virgin. I saw a nook in his backyard, where daisies and lilies and tulips flourished. They were bright pink, blue, and red. Growing next to them were garlic, sweet green peppers, fresh basil. Sweet red vine tomatoes, the best I'd ever tasted, sliced and spread across homemade toast. He tended to the garden, wearing a sunhat to protect his chestnut eyes. Now, his eyes deep as caves hollowed out his face, telling stories of World War II, stationed off the coast of Honolulu when the Japanese invaded Pearl Harbor. They told stories of my grandmother sending him photos of herself, wearing grass skirts and leis, and of him proposing to her on the beach. They told the story leading up to mourning a child lost to heroin, the only time I saw him cry openly, loud and hard. Growing old and letting go.

It neared five o'clock in the morning, and Krista and I sprawled on the bed, our heads where feet typically rest. Dozing off and waking up, our calves dangled off the side of the comforter. Nanu's head jerked forward. "Ugggh...." He choked on the brownish yellow bile, now actual pieces of collapsing esophagus. As it rose up into his throat, Krista jumped up and grabbed the bucket for him to spit in. We'd been doing this on and off through the night. During intervals, we relaxed in the same positions, but Lisa was the most awake, still on West Coast time.

"Here, Gina, hold this in front of him," Krista said, handing me the bucket. She stumbled over to his right side, lifting his arm and shoulder, pulling him up higher. Lisa held his other side, and together they helped him sit up more to alleviate the acidic burning. Lisa dropped the hard covered book again, this time letting its thin sheets flutter. My sisters bolstered him, each grabbing hold of an elbow. I reached the bucket toward his mouth. My hand trembled; I felt like I wasn't getting close enough, but I couldn't. I was trying to lean over the length of his body, without falling on him, without hurting him. I felt guilty being barely able to look at his unrecognizable physique. But if I looked at him, I'd break again and again. I'd only upset him.

He continued to release the bile, loud now, choking. His body turned paste colored. His vocal cords hushed. With the end of the noise, his eyes rolled upward, high into his head, and then shut, his arms stretched out toward my sisters. His face pointed straight ahead toward me. I was still gripping the bucket, trying not to drop it on him. I wanted to close my eyes, but I couldn't—I couldn't leave—even though his skin wasn't his own, and his face not mine anymore, not ours. I didn't look at my sisters, but I knew they hadn't moved. It was as if our pulses had stopped too, the weight of our blood high up in our throats. It was as if time had stopped. The three of us were still, an intricate diamond bound by our four bodies.

Transit

Evan Lottich

Cars got going
When Mom and Dad were dating.
I came in time to ride along
In the bright new yellow Ford
With folding top
That took us once on gravel
All the way from Iowa to Indiana
So Dad could show me off to Gramp.
When I got way up to five
I'd shout the name of every passing make.
Franklin! Pierce-Arrow! Oakland!
Back then some cars
You cranked the windshield up
To get a breeze.
Today what do I know?
Last car the air thing quit
And too much else.
I don't have many places to go
But I do have this new walker now
I want to paintbrush yellow.

Prepare

KC Eib

Mark the metal box in soot.

Chiseled bones ship alongside petrified wood.

Do not call names of un-mouthed faces.

Shave casings with a dead man's razor.

Drink his ocean from a bamboo straw.

Plant a leather shoe till it sun-bakes to creases.

Vacuum leaves from canopies.

Uncoil the umbilical cord in cinnamon strips.

Boil light in the bottoms of your eyes.

Songs hang on a midnight wire.

Buy a ticket and wait.

Line the lids in steel.

Drown the deciduous welcome.

Do not waver.

Embrace his body.

Bury words in red dirt.

Shoreline

John Kristofco

like love
the sea is mute,
imprisoned in its depth
beneath the moon,

anguished in its limits,
thrashing for the soul of the horizon,
thinned to eddies,
pools in the sand

embarrassed by
the simple light of day

All of the Above

Rob E. Boley

To properly support the head and neck, an effective pillow will maintain a height of approximately five inches.

This is the first thought to go through Larry's alcohol-scorched mind on Saturday morning, and he has no idea where the thought came from. It's true, of course, and his pillow is anything but effective, proper, or supportive. In fact, right now his pillow is, in fact, a running shoe.

He sits up, stares at his shoe. Rubs his aching neck.

Slowly, he realizes that someone is watching him. It's his nine-year-old son Patrick, whose attention is torn between what's on TV (Spider-Man beating up a giant lizard) and what's on the family room floor (Larry).

"Hey, buddy," says Larry. "Daddy was just camping out on the floor. Practicing for, uh, camping."

"Are we going camping?"

"Um. Eventually?"

"What about snakes? I'm afraid of snakes."

"There are only about 8,000 venomous snakebites in this entire country, buddy, and no more than a dozen fatalities annually. That's .0025 of a percent of the population." The stats and calculations tumble over Larry's tongue, and again he has no idea where the facts come from.

Patrick cocks his head toward his father, though his gaze is fixated on the television. "That doesn't help, Dad."

Using all of his available stamina, energy, and coordination, Larry walks into the kitchen, sits down at the breakfast table, and closes his eyes. The darkness there, normally comforting, is tainted by the unpleasant sensation that starved maggots are gnawing at the backs of his eyelids. Larry opens his eyes, his groggy vision settling on the already open morning paper.

Larry's wife, Gail, stands over the stove tending to a pan of scrambled eggs. Not looking at him. "What time did you get home last night?"

Larry closes his eyes, preferring at least for the moment to face the hungry maggots. "Why do you ask me what time I got in, when you know already?"

"Because I want to see if you were too drunk to know."

"Fine. It was three o'clock." She stares at him blankly. "Four o'clock." More staring. "Half past four?"

Gail turns back to the stove, stirs the eggs. "How much did you have to drink?"

"Um, more than enough."

"What if you'd gotten into an accident? What if you'd killed yourself, or someone else?"

Gail audibly grits her teeth, and he cringes. Not because he has a problem with teeth-gritting, but because Gail looks like her mother when she grits.

"You shouldn't put milk in with the eggs," says Larry. "It makes them burn. Use a bit of water instead."

She stares at him now, while the eggs behind her smolder. "What? You're the cook now?"

"Sorry. I guess I must have read that somewhere." But did he? No. He has no idea where this cooking knowledge came from. He turns the page of the paper, hoping for an interesting article to change the subject. Instead he finds an article about the renovation of a local building, which contains a fact—that the building was built in 1934—that he somehow knows to be untrue.

What. The. Hell?

At the end of the paper is the crossword. Gail has entered three of the answers before giving up. He picks up a pen, stares at the blank little squares on the page. A five-letter word for trout basket: Creel. A six-letter expression of annoyance: Tsk-tsk. A seven-letter word that makes animals' eyes shine in the dark.

"Tapetum?" says Larry.

"What?" asks Gail, dumping the eggs into the wastebasket.

"Tapetum. It's what makes animals eyes glow."

"Uh-huh."

A five-letter word for a dispatch boat. A ten-letter breed of dog. An eleven-letter Latin illogical conclusion. Aviso. Rottweiler. Non sequitur.

On and on it goes until Larry finishes the entire puzzle. When he places his pen down, he is stunned with silence. He moves on to yesterday's crossword, filling in the answers almost unconsciously while Gail whips up a new batch of eggs.

"Whoa, check out the brain on Dad," says Patrick, standing behind Larry.

"Not bad, huh, kiddo?"

Patrick sits next to Larry, and Gail places a fresh plate of eggs in front of him. She leans over Larry, mouthing the answers to the crossword.

"How did you know all of this?" she asks.

Larry shrugs. "I just...I just did."

Patrick puts down his fork. "Mom, these are the best eggs ever."

"Thanks," she says, sighing. "I used water instead of milk."

"We'll need to drive separately to Mom's," says Gail, later that morning. "I'm bringing over that table from the garage."

"That's today, isn't it?" says Larry, who is now lying on the couch drinking an odd-smelling mixture.

"I figured I'd go over early to spend some time with her," says Gail. "So you can wait until closer to dinner."

"No, that's okay. I'll just leave at the same time."

This is typical, and it frustrates Gail beyond belief. Larry knows he'll have a bad time, but he goes anyway, out of some retarded sense of duty to Gail. But his being at Mom's practically pouting only serves to irritate Gail. And speaking of irritating...

She wrinkles her nose. "What are you drinking?"

He holds up the glass. "Pickle juice. Orange juice. Gatorade. Tomato juice. Hot sauce. Coffee."

"Why?"

"To cure my..." His eyes flick to Patrick, who is flipping through the channels. "My cold. I've got a whopper of a headache."

Patrick looks over. "I'm guessing all the drinking didn't help your cold, Dad."

Great. Gail picks up the drink, sniffs. Retches. "And where did you get the idea for this unholy concoction?"

"It just occurred to me." The TV catches his interest and he sits up quickly. "Buddy, leave it here a second."

"*Fill in the Blank?*" asks Patrick.

"Just for a minute."

"Okay, contestants," says the well-manicured host on the screen. "Welcome back to *Fill in the Blank*. It's time for the Final Blanks. Whoever gets the most correct answers, wins the round. Ready?" The contestants nod.

"Blank predicted that Jesus was going to be born in Bethlehem."

"Micah," answers Larry, just before one of the contestants.

"Correct," says the host.

"Blank contains all five vowels in reverse alphabetical order."

"Subcontinental and Unoriental," answers Larry.

Seconds later, the female contestant answers, "Subcontinental."

"Correct," responds the host. "We also would have accepted 'unoriental.' "

Patrick looks up at his dad, eyes and mouth wide open. Larry glances down at his son and smiles nervously. Gail just shakes her head. Something's up. Larry isn't a stupid man. He's remarkably clever and creative, in fact, but he's never been good with facts. She can easily trounce him in Trivial Pursuit or Scrabble.

"In the nation of Blank, the Indus River flows into the ocean," says the host.

"Pakistan," says Larry, then turning to Gail: "How did I know that? I couldn't even tell you where Pakistan is on a map." Larry pauses, closes his eyes. "Oh, wait. Yeah, I guess I can."

Gail shakes her head. She can't let this distract her from the topic at hand, not when she still has an ace in the hole. "Instead of going to Mom's early, you could always finish painting the garage."

"Not if it's going to rain," responds Larry.

"If you don't want to do it, just say so. Have you been outside today? There isn't a cloud in the sky."

"It's going to rain," says Larry. "I'm sure of it."

"The paper said it'd be clear all weekend."

"The paper's wrong. Believe me. I read the whole thing, and I spotted several other bits of misinformation."

"Yeah. I bet you did."

Later, Larry is still in the recliner, now watching a historical documentary about the Civil War.

"Well, they got that part all wrong," says Larry, shaking his head.

"We're leaving," says Gail abruptly from the kitchen. "I'll see you over there."

"Do you need help with the table?" asks Larry, getting out of his chair.

"That's okay," says Gail, though her tone indicated that it clearly is not. She slams the side door as she and Patrick exit through the kitchen.

Larry grunts. "God. Damn. It."

He stomps to the bedroom, changes quickly out of his pajamas. As he slides into his jeans, he marvels at the fact that one bale of cotton can produce a whopping 215 pairs of jeans. The official birthday of blue jeans is May 20th, also the date in 1570 that cartographer Abraham Ortelius created the first modern-day atlas. The dye used most commonly for jeans is phthalocyanine, an intensely colored macrocyclic compound with low solubility in virtually all solvents. As potential cancer-fighting properties of phthalocyanine cells flitter across Larry's consciousness, he clenches his teeth and growls. Takes a deep breath.

On his way out the door, he actually finds his car keys right where he expects them to be—an event that hasn't happened in years.

His Camry zips along the side streets of their neighborhood. Gail will take the highway, but the back roads will be faster. Veering the car onto County Road 19, he pulls out his cell phone, dials his friend Todd Leone.

Todd picks up, his voice raw. "Why, man? Why so early?"

"Todd, did you know that your Italian surname is derived from the Latin *leonis*, a nickname for a fierce or brave warrior? Did you know that you share said surname with a Canadian businessman and criminal, an Italian long-distance runner, a food critic, a Canadian model, and a film director? Did you know all that, Todd? Because I sure as hell do. What the hell happened last night? I can't remember anything after the nacho dip."

"Hold on, Wiki-Larry. What the hell, man? I just woke up."

"Just tell me what we did last night."

"I dunno. Got pretty crazy. We mixed a bunch of crazy new drinks with shit Kevin found in his freezer. We played online video games with strangers. We had a Dorito-eating contest sometime after midnight. Oh, and we microwaved Scott's broken iPhone. That shit was hilarious."

"Uh-huh. Anything else?"

"Think that about covers it."

Larry sighs. "Thanks, Todd. I'll catch you later. Hey, don't forget that the *Beverly Hills 90210* marathon starts at five o'clock."

"Thanks. Hey, how did you know that I watch *90210*?"

"I wish I knew."

Larry clicks off. His car speeds past stretches of leafy trees, and then past acres of cornfields. The long stalks blur together as Larry picks up speed. There are about 795 kernels in 16 rows on each ear of corn. Wonderful to know.

Larry has never been one for excessive speed, but today he knows exactly how fast he can accelerate into a turn without skidding off the road. As he zips around a bend at a swift 72 miles per hour, his head flashes with approximations of entry, apex, exit, weight, velocity, friction, braking point, and wind resistance.

And then the rain starts.

When Gail pulls their squat CRV into her mother's driveway, Larry's Camry is already sitting next to the garage. Larry is still behind the wheel, and Gail wonders how long he's waited there and why. Because he wants to see her face when she sees that he beat her there, or because he hates being alone with his mother-in-law, or because he wants to gloat about the rain? Likely all of the above.

Stepping onto the wet driveway, he smiles and waves as Patrick exits the CRV.

"Dad, how did you get here so fast?"

"I took the back roads," he says.

"You?" says Gail, stepping into the misty rain. "You get lost going through the drive-thru. You never take the back roads."

"Well, today I did. I knew the way, and I knew it'd be faster." Larry pauses. "And I wanted to help you with the table."

Gail feels her lips stretching into a smile. "Thanks."

The Belanger house, where Gail had grown up, is much larger than Larry and Gail's house. Located in one of the older suburbs around town, a neighborhood built when it first became fashionable for the wealthy to live outside of the downtown area, it boasts the most immaculate garden on the street.

"Hi, Mom," yells Gail, as she and Larry maneuver the table into the house. Patrick holds open the front door.

"Careful with that," snaps her mom, Samia. Her blond hair is pulled up into a neat little bun, her nails are manicured, and her makeup is heavy but impeccable. "You didn't use a blanket to move it? I hope it's not scuffed."

With that, Mom turns on her heel and returns to the kitchen. Larry and Gail exchange glances, and she's struck by a gleam in his eye—something she hasn't seen since...ever?

"Smells good, Mom," says Larry, following her into the kitchen.

Mom cringes slightly at the sound of Larry using the word "Mom" at her. She stands over the stove, stirring a pot of vegetable soup. The kitchen is spotless, even the presumably dirty coffee cup in the sink gleams.

"Thank you, Lawrence," she says.

"The garden looks great," says Gail, sitting down at the kitchen table. It will win neighborhood pride awards—yet again.

"Patrick," says Samia, "why don't you go out to the garden and get some carrots for the salad?"

"Sure, Grandma."

Gail grabs a piece of celery and fills a glass of water from the tap. She pulls the ice tray out of the freezer and slams it hard on the counter. A few blocks of ice leap out of the tray, as if startled. She drops them into her glass.

"Are you still *trying* to lose weight, Gail?" asks Samia, watching as Gail munches on the celery.

"Yeah, I'd like to lose a few more pounds."

"You know that's just an old wives' tale," says Samia, refilling the ice tray and sliding it back in the freezer. "Drinking ice water doesn't really burn calories."

"Actually, that's not true," says Larry. "If you drink a sixteen-ounce glass of ice water, your system has to raise the temperature of the water from zero to thirty-seven degrees. To do that, you probably burn about seventeen calories. Now, that might not sound like much, but multiple that by the eight glasses of water that Gail likely drinks per day, and it could be as much as 136 calories. That's about what she'd burn walking for a half hour a day. It's just shy of a thousand calories a week."

"Thank you, Lawrence. Your insight is appreciated." Samia looks back at Gail. "That was the great thing about your father. He knew when to keep his mouth shut."

"Ben was a great guy," says Larry, "but he spent his whole life terrified of you. No matter what he did, it was never good enough. Right up until he had his stroke, he was just trying to do the impossible: make you happy. And Gail has fallen into the same trap. She will always be too fat or too thin. Patrick will never be smart enough and well-mannered enough. And I'm never going to measure up to the husband that you sent to the grave."

Gail is mortified, though every word Larry says is true. Her mother grits her teeth, which is even more mortifying because Gail knows she does the exact same thing. Gail takes one last bite of celery and walks out of the room, leaving Larry and Mom alone.

"These carrots are huge!" says Patrick, walking into the kitchen with an armful of carrots, the first vegetable to be canned commercially. Native to Afghanistan, this biennial plant has a flowering stem whose flowers produce a mericarp, a type of dry fruit.

Patrick is oblivious to the wall of silence that had arisen between Larry and Samia. Larry takes Patrick's arrival as a cue to leave.

"Pat, help your grandma with the carrots."

Larry walks briskly out of the kitchen, finds Gail in the upstairs
bathroom. He doesn't bother trying the knob, knows it's locked. He
knocks three times on the door, asks, "Can I come in, babe?"

The doorknob clicks. Gail is standing at the sink, gazing at her
reflection in the spotless mirror.

"I'm sorry," he says. "I shouldn't have said that."

"It was all true."

"Well, that doesn't mean it needed said. I'm sorry. I've been Mr.
Know-It-All all day, and it kind of went to my head. I've been kinda
arrogant."

She smirks playfully. "Kinda?"

He steps behind her, wrapping his arms around her waist and
hugging her tight. They stare at themselves in the mirror. For over a
dozen years they've been married. They've eaten countless meals (817,
actually), rode hundreds of thousands of miles, watched weeks' worth
of television, shared thousands of kisses—all together. The weight of
these statistics makes his vision blur. Larry squeezes his eyes shut and
refocuses on his wife's reflection. He sees her: the truth of her, not the
image of her that's been molded and baked inside his head.

"You're beautiful."

"Thank you."

"I'm sorry about staying out so late," he says.

"You can stay out all night and I wouldn't care. I just don't want
you driving in that condition."

"It was stupid. I'm sorry."

"So, were there any hot girls at the bar last night," she asks, rock-
ing gently back and forth, so that her backside rubs against his crotch.

"None as hot as you," says Larry, kissing her lightly on the back
of the neck.

She cocks her head so that he can kiss her behind the ear—her favorite spot. He squeezes her waist and continues kissing. Her body still facing the mirror, Gail cranes her neck to kiss his lips.

After three minutes and thirty seconds of kissing, in which they each burn 91 calories, use all 34 facial muscles, and swap 57 million colonies of bacteria, Larry drops his hand into the waistband of her skirt.

"Larry, this isn't...don't..."

She stops herself as Larry's fingertips explore her. He's never been very good with his hands, but suddenly finds himself expertly rubbing and touching Gail. She closes her eyes and lifts her skirt, moans.

"Don't stop kissing my neck."

Gail almost slips into dreamscape—a rain-spotted canvas of undulating bushes and quivering flowers —but the tremors inside her body continually snap her back to consciousness.

"You were snoring," says Larry, sprawled out on the bathroom mat with Gail's upper body draped across his chest.

"Dammit. We didn't use any protection."

Larry pats her back. Those hands. Oh, my God, those hands. "You ovulated nine days ago, hon. We should be safe."

Gail does some math in her head, smiles. "What's gotten into you today? How are you suddenly so different?"

"I don't know. I just know all these things that I didn't know before. Like how to find Pakistan. Or your g-spot. I think...I think I know everything. I mean, not at once. But all day long, every piece of information I need, every question I have...it all just comes to me. Sometimes when I don't want it, too."

"Oh, whatever," says Gail, playfully biting his hairy chest.

Larry jumps. "I'm not kidding. Try me. Ask me anything."

"Okay, what is the name of Jupiter's largest moon?"

"Ganymede. But you wouldn't have known if that was right or wrong."

Gail bites her lip, sits up, and grabs her mother's deodorant from out of a drawer. "Okay, smarty-pants, tell me the ingredients in this."

"You realize that your mom rubs that in her armpit, right?"

"The ingredients, Larry."

"Active or inactive?"

"Inactive."

"Cyclopentasiloxane, stearyl alcohol, cyclohexasiloxane, PPG-14 butyl ether, phenyl—"

"Okay, enough," says Gail, her eyes wide with amazement. This was starting to scare her. Was there something wrong with Larry's brain? A tumor? "How the hell did you do that?"

Larry shrugs. "It just came to me."

"No, I mean how the hell did you know how to pronounce cyclo..." She squints closer at the list of ingredients. "Cyclopenta..."

"Cyclopentasiloxane," finishes Larry. "It's an odorless, silicone fluid also known as cyclic pentamer. Melts at negative 44 degrees Celsius. Boils at 90 degrees." He grabs the deodorant, runs his finger down the small print. "I know the same information for all of these, plus a couple ingredients that conveniently weren't listed here. Huh."

"You're starting to creep me out," says Gail, pulling her panties on. "We should go back out there. God knows what my mom must think."

"That we had hot, wild sex in her bathroom?"

"Exactly," says Gail, smacking Larry's thigh. "Let's go." As Larry stands, Gail considers the day's events, puts her hand on Larry's shoulder. "Okay, here's a question. What's the meaning of life?"

Larry pauses. He opens his mouth, as if about to speak, then closes it again. Looks upward, as if the answer is hiding beneath his eyelids or at the fringe of his frontal lobe. "An organismic state identified with growth, reproduction, metabolism, and reaction to stimuli?" Larry shakes his head. "No, that's not what you mean, is it? I…I don't know."

"Ha," says Gail. "Guess you don't know everything after all."

After an awkward but delicious dinner, Larry helps Patrick into the CRV, making sure that he is buckled in securely. Gail kisses him on the back of the neck, her lips as light as butterfly wings, made of thin layers of hardened protein called chitin covered with thousands of miniature scales and hairs called setae.

"Hey," she says, "take those back roads and show me how you got here so fast, okay?"

"Okay."

He climbs into his Camry and backs out of the driveway, still pondering Gail's question. What is the meaning of life? Butterfly wings. Tapetum. An atlas. Melting point. Snake venom. Water and eggs. Subcontinental. Ice melting in a belly. Dried fruit. It's all connected somehow…

Several miles later, he is back on Country Road 19, surrounded by flickering stalks of corn now wet with rain and glistening like jewels in the bright sun.

"If I know everything," reasons Larry aloud, "yet I don't know the meaning of life, then it follows that life has no meaning." Larry pauses, taking in this full weight of this insight. "Bummer." But no, that's not quite right.

He looks in the rearview mirror to make sure Gail is still following behind. She is. His eyes flick back to the road.

Three quarters of a mile ahead, a big, red pickup truck comes from the opposite direction. All last night and into morning, the driver of the truck played an online role-playing game, slaying hundreds of ogres and orcs. Larry knows this. The man is nodding off, snug in a ray of sunshine. Larry knows this. On its present course, the truck is going to drift over the yellow line and run into Gail's CRV. It's all physics, probability, and geometry. A seamless calculation of velocities, momentum, impact, weights, and measures. The truck is going to kill his family.

Larry knows this.

He beeps his horn. The old and rusted Ford, its gnarled grill the final resting place for hundreds of bugs, keeps on coming, its driver-side tires inching toward the worn yellow line. The driver's head nods downward.

Taking a deep breath, Larry cuts the wheel hard to the left, hitting the truck almost dead on with a jarring crash. Larry's Camry tumbles across the road and through a buckshot-riddled speed limit sign. The rusty metal of the sign tears through the car, slicing into Larry's air bag and into Larry's gut. A wet slap of pain.

The car finally comes to rest sideways in a ditch on the opposite side of the road. Still strapped in by his seat belt, Larry hangs downward, which in this case, is toward the passenger side of the car. Looking down, he watches his small intestine, twenty feet long, spill out of his body onto the passenger's seat.

Duodenum. Jejunum. Ileum. Epithelial tissue. Mucosa. Plicae circulares. It takes about eight hours for food to pass through the stomach and small intestine. By a coincidence Larry is only beginning to understand, that's about how long he's been awake today.

He tries calling for Gail, sprays blood over the steering wheel.

"Stay here," she tells Patrick, slamming her door closed. "Close your eyes."

She runs toward the Camry lying sideways in the ditch. Directly in her path is the driver of the truck—lying in the road at the end of a trail of blood and gore, his arm twisted and broken behind his neck. He screams at her for help, his jaw hanging crooked like a door half off its hinges.

Standing over him, Gail pulls out her phone. No signal. She pulls out her wallet, though she's not sure why. "I'm...I'm sorry..." she says, dropping her driver's license next to the man. "I have to go."

Even several steps away, she hears Larry's ragged breathing—like someone sucking air through a damp sponge. When she reaches the ditch, she vomits bits of soup and salad into the wet grass. Wiping bits of carrot from her mouth, she puts a hand on the Camry.

The ditch is deep enough that she's able to bend over the edge of the car and reach into Larry's broken side window. Her husband stares up at her, and her heart squirms into her belly. Oh, God. Larry. So much blood.

He reaches for her, and she grabs his bloody hand. "Larry," she says. "I'm here. I'm right here."

He stares at her, his eyes remarkably focused. "Patrick?"

"He's okay." She squeezes his hand. "What happened, Larry? Was there an animal in the road? Did a tire blow? Did you lose control?"

"The answer's..." he starts, closing his eyes and smiling. He coughs, takes his last breath. "All of the above."

Night Hike

Marilyn Ringer

Her lantern doused, the starlit trail well-known, she stepped into
    dark's hand.
He thumbed her arch.

One moment standing, one moment down, turned on the hereditary
    loose ankle.
A dancer's foot, had she been taller

or had loved Mrs. Helvey's class, where she pliéd in the back row,
an awkward duckling among swans.

Lying on the path, she laughed, took it as a caution.
The moon set its orange belly in the sea.

The World Gets Easier

Yvonne Higgins Leach

We are the last patrons
at Mary's open-air restaurant

in Colimilla, Mexico.
Everyone else sobered up

on the water taxi back to Barra
across the lagoon. We order

barbequed shrimp stuffed
with cheese I don't buy in America

and again sit back under the roof
layered with palm fronds, and with each

margarita the world gets easier.
Our troubles are north of this border,

where the air is cold and we live
with our adult responsibilities. For now

our mouths one moment smack
with the tart of lime,

and the next smooth out from the
sweet touch of agave nectar,

and the air is warm around our shoulders.

September's Skin

Jean Howard

I should write a poem
while I'm here
and September's skin
is still tanned
and sweeping as arms
up the hill,

While the bees still drift,
pockets of gold
at each heel,

While shadows still tip
gracefully into each
crease, stone
or flower,
and the sun slips
down earlier,

And I still have words,
outside,

hardening to chestnut,
but inside,
still tender with
meat.

The Art of the Drop Kick

Rudy Dicks

I never doubted Spyder Pollett when he told me he could drop kick a football 51 yards. No, not for an instant. I only wondered why anyone would want to do such a thing.

I admit I did not know all that much about it. I liked football. And I thought I knew the game as well as—maybe better than—the average fan. I knew that pro players could kick that far; even good college kickers could. I knew that records for field goals were longer, maybe by 5, 10 yards even, but the exact distance? Who knows how far? But Spyder corrected me. I had missed the point.

"No," he said, smiling, raising his index finger like a parent gently correcting a child. "I'm talking about the drop kick. It's an entirely different thing"

Slowly, I remembered. Tucked away in my memory was the flicker of one of those old newsreels, so grainy and herky-jerky that I could practically hear the clattering of the projector in my head. I could see football players from the 1920s grinning, hands on hips as they posed with the self-confidence of kids who believed they could outrun, out-jump, out-muscle any obstacle the world threw at them, looking as if they would always stay as young and fresh as their college yearbook photos. And in my mind was a flash of a player cradling a football, pausing before he took two or three steps and let the ball slide from his hands, simple as an acorn falling from a tree, then snapping his leg forward and kicking the lumpy ball at the exact moment it tapped off the ground, propelling his body up like a padded dancer in search of an invisible step.

I couldn't recall exactly. Maybe I hadn't seen a film. Maybe I was just imagining the scene. But I thought no one could ever do that with a sleek, modern football, aerodynamically designed for throwing like a dart. I knew that much. I'd played enough touch football to know that you could never get a perfect bounce from the pointy noses of these footballs and time your kick to greet the ball perfectly with your toe. You'd be lucky just to nick the football with your foot, leaving the ball feebly squirting and twitching as it hopped off the ground like a crippled windup toy.

"You heard of George Gipp of Notre Dame, haven't you?" Spyder said.

"Sure. 'Win one for The Gipper,' right?"

"He drop kicked a 62-yarder one time, November 11, 1916, against Western Michigan. He was on the freshman team at Notre Dame. 62 yards."

The thought conjured up images of college kids from a century ago, lined up in team photos as if they fit together as naturally as a family portrait at a holiday dinner. Arms crossed and fists tucked snugly under their armpits, shoulders pooched, slick hair oiled and parted neatly in the middle, most looking as serious as men going off to war, one or two squelching a snicker, as if privy to a practical joke. I saw floppy, beaten-up leather helmets with no face masks, almost like the helmets of World War I pilots in open cockpits, black high-topped cleats, and a ball-carrier soaring through the air, smirking while stiff-arming an imaginary tackler. I pictured a balloon of a football, plump and misshapen as a pumpkin that hangs on too long after Halloween, clutched inside an arm covered by a scratchy-looking, woolen jersey with striped sleeves and patches that fought to keep the shirt from unraveling.

"I know it sounds funny," Spyder said, scuffing the toe of his shoe in the grass and squinting against the noon autumn sun. "Can't blame you if you don't believe me. I wouldn't blame anyone for not believing me. Who's ever seen anyone drop kick a football nowadays?"

It's not like I could have asked Spyder to prove it right then and there, in the middle of the quadrangle on campus, even if that's the kind of dare you can't resist whether you're a middle school kid or a college senior. But Spyder was the one person, I thought, who could look dignified, utterly free of self-consciousness no matter what unreasonable position you stuck him in, even as others might gape at him. So I had to smile at the thought of Spyder maneuvering through the students lounging on the grass, a puffed-up ball clasped gingerly between his hands, then chugging a few steps before whoompfff!, sending that ball end over end, with as smooth and symmetrical and leisurely a backspin as the flapping wings of a bird, with the same carefree flight that could keep it soaring endlessly. I had a flicker of a fantasy, watching the students' gaze as the ball climbed as if it were in slow motion, ascending toward an unknown destination, then drifting down like a kid's kite, exhausted by the energy to stay aloft. I imagined the sharp echo knifing the silence as the ball landed with a splat! on the sidewalk, then waggling with a couple drunken bounces before rolling to a stop.

What a delightful lark that would be. How easy it is to make people shrink back at something so harmless yet foreign to them, so fearsome, only because they didn't understand it. But I preferred to think they would all suddenly explode in unison with cheers and frantic clapping, not because it was a great athletic feat, but a magical act. I ducked my head to hide my grin.

Spyder scooted up onto the backrest of the bench as I leaned forward to escape his shadow. The days were clinging to shreds of the sun's warmth, but fall was impatient and jittery and ready to flee. And as I watched leaves on the maple trees waddle down like they were landing by parachute, I couldn't help but mentally pace off 50 yards. Or 51.

Spyder's arm almost grazed my head as he swung it to point in front of me. "See there?" he asked. "From the blonde in the black turtleneck to the statue of that guy looks like he's inviting a lady to dance. From her," he said, moving his finger left to right and back, "to that statue. 50 yards."

I looked at the girl clutching her books, arms wrapped in front of her chest, talking to an English professor I had my sophomore year. Then I looked at the mottled green statue, dappled with bird droppings, like spilled paint. I crooked my neck to look up at Spyder. "Wherever would you get one of those fat old footballs to kick anyway, Spyder? They don't make those anymore. They don't exist. Maybe in the farthest corner of someone's grandfather's attic." *Or someone's memory*, I thought.

Spyder had a limber body, about 6-foot-2, with shoulders that fanned out like the hood of a cobra, and arms and legs that flexed with muscle like a greyhound and swiveled with a geometric precision. His body was all angles and movements that were smooth but not mechanical, that had no wasted motion. He had a narrow face with thin lips and a sharp triangle of a nose that, combined with his shaggy crew cut, gave him the appearance of some sort of bird, hawk-like, but softened by his gray eyes.

Spyder stroked his mouth at the corners and shook his head. "I don't need one of those old-fashioned footballs. Just give me a football. Any ball."

Spyder had the look of an athlete, to be sure, but you couldn't size him up and match him to a sport. I had no doubt those legs could whip into a ball and kick it half the length of a football field, but I couldn't see how anyone could drop a pointy ball and make it bounce so true that you could kick it accurately. Like trying to drop a bullet and have it bounce straight up. And time it so that you connected at the split-second after it kissed the ground.

I'd heard different stories about Spyder Pollett. Someone told me that before transferring, he had gone to college in Kansas for a year. Or maybe it was Missouri. After that he tried a junior college, and then dropped out. He worked for a year or two at a couple jobs, fighting forest fires out west, then working on a freighter hauling iron ore out of Duluth. That seemed like an exotic world, and it filled me with wonder, thinking of a guy barely older than me but years more worldly crossing one of the Great Lakes on a ship the length of a football field, rolling on huge waves in slow motion as lightning zapped the sky.

I wondered what it was like to stand on a ship in the middle of a lake so vast it might as well be the ocean, in complete darkness, as if the rest of the world had forgotten all about you. I gushed at Spyder during lunch one day that he could handle the kinds of jobs that none of the rest of us would ever tackle once we graduated. He shrugged. "That really wasn't what I was looking for," he said. "I took what I could get. I really didn't have much choice."

Spyder rested his forearms on the cafeteria table and leaned toward me. "You know what I really wanted to do?" he asked, almost in a whisper, grinning broadly. "What I really wanted to be? I'll tell you: A lighthouse keeper. Up on the Great Lakes. Someplace where they get furious storms—the kind that swoop in with clouds the color of black-and-blue-and-purple bruises. The kind that could beat you down with fear. I worked on a ship, yeah, but I wanted to be the one to guide the ships and make sure they got through safely. I could do that. I know I could."

"But you couldn't get a job at a lighthouse?"

Spyder eased back in his chair, stretching his legs out. "The Coast Guard took control of them years ago," he said. "They still run some. A lot of the lighthouses are automated now. They don't need humans. Some are only museums, and some have been abandoned. There are barely any left with real lighthouse keepers."

"Too bad. For you, I mean. I guess you came along too late."

"Captains of ships used to get those jobs," he said. "And if the guy died, maybe the wife would take over the post. Sometimes it was politics, giving the job to a friend. I stopped once at a lighthouse and asked a couple Coast Guard guys, how could I get that job? I'd work for free. They could train me. I could learn, I know that. Just let me try. Gimme a chance. Know what they said? They said maybe I should enlist. They thought that was pretty funny."

I had heard Spyder was a pretty good football player in high school, but he never got a major college offer, no big-time scholarship. It was Bruno who told me how Spyder tried to win a spot on his college team as a freshman. A walk-on. Kansas, was it? Bruno knew him because they'd gone to the same high school, a few years apart.

"See, Spyder talked an assistant coach into giving him a try-out," Bruno said, tapping his finger on the table. "Well, sort of. Most people would start with a polite introduction, right? But Spyder likes to plunge into things. So he goes to the practice field, waits till the end of practice, then grabs the top of this 6-foot fence surrounding the field and leaps over, when the only people left were an assistant coach and a player—a punter—standing at midfield, getting in some final kicks. Spyder walks over in his street clothes, that easy smile on his face, you know? The coach, he just stares at him. 'I'm a kicker,' Spyder says. You picture this? Spyder introducing himself like he's running for mayor? And he points to the ball in the coach's hands, then to the goalposts, and says, 'I can nail that from 50 yards.'"

Bruno shook his head. "Still the coach doesn't say anything. But he flips Spyder the ball, figures it'll be more fun to watch the kid make a fool of himself than to just run him off, right? Like you humor someone you think is crazy. Spyder snatches the ball, doesn't even take off his jacket, measures his steps, takes a few strides, and then, just like he says, bang! Nails it. A 40-yard drop kick. Not 50, ok? But 40."

I thought again of Spyder in the quadrangle, and I licked my lips and felt one of my eyelids twitch. Bruno tilted his head back, smiled, and slowly twirled his bare hands in front of him.

"So, the coach watches the ball sail through the uprights, it comes spinning down and bounces off the ground. Guy doesn't say a word, right? The punter, he's watching all this, he goes, 'Sonuvabitch.' The coach, he's still staring at the uprights. Then he grabs another ball off the ground, flips it to Spyder, says, 'Do that again.' Spyder takes a couple steps and drop kicks it from 45 yards this time. Coach watches the ball go through the uprights, shakes his head, and asks, 'What's your name, son?' Spyder answers, 'Pollett. It's Puh-LETT, sort of like you'd say 'polite.' The coach sighs and says, 'Kid, that's one helluva trick.' And he walks away."

Bruno shook his head and stared at the floor. "Swear to God, that's the way Spyder told me. You know—after I kept quizzing him about it. You know how he is. By then I guess even he thought it had turned into a joke. But that was the end of Spyder's tryout. And his football career."

Saturdays in the fall, Spyder would come to the home football games to watch with the rest of us, but he never arrived before kickoff. He'd show up near the end of the first quarter, then he'd get restless and drift off halfway through the fourth quarter, even if it was a close game. He would just say, "Gotta go." Sometimes you'd look around and he was gone. Just like that. Maybe small-college football wasn't that exciting to him. Maybe he'd seen enough football. I don't know.

I remember how he tried to explain football to Sofia. Nice kid. He liked her, and he didn't even mind that she thought the game was pointless. She had an obsession with ballet and dance, and she only came to this one game. Spyder tried to explain kicking a field goal to her. "Kick a ball through those Popsicle sticks and you get three points?" she asked with a trace of a smile. "What's the sense of that?" That was as much as Spyder tried to explain football to her. Or get to know her.

Spyder was a couple years older than me, but he was more than a year behind me in credits for graduation. I always figured that he lagged behind because of the time he was out of school and the credits he had lost when he transferred, but then I discovered it was because he had changed his mind about his major so often. I had assumed that because I rarely saw him with books he wasn't much of a student, but that wasn't it. Bruno said that Spyder was the same way in high school. Never saw Spyder with books, but Spyder was in the top five of his class. I was wrong about a few things about Spyder.

I asked Spyder about drop kicking one more time, when I ran into him sitting on the steps of the library in April. Somehow I couldn't get the idea out of my head, like one of those puzzles with movable pieces you have to maneuver into some position.

"There was a time that was a thing of beauty," Spyder said. "It was a specialized skill, something people who played the game respected. Shoot, it was more than that. It was a weapon. Nobody remembers now, but it had a great tradition. Look at Charlie Brickley of Harvard. He beat Yale, single-handed, 1913, five field goals on drop kicks. Beat Princeton, 3–0, same year. They say he and Jim Thorpe held kicking contests at halftime of games, after they went pro.

"Mickey Cochrane, the catcher, baseball Hall of Famer? He had a 52-yard drop kick for Boston University against Brown, 1923. Good athlete like that, I guess it doesn't surprise you. That same year, Jack Pence of Coe, he drop kicks a 59-yarder against Drake."

Spyder poked my arm and laughed out loud. "Man, imagine what it must feel like to drop kick a ball 59 yards."

I raised my palms in the air weakly and shook my head.

"You think it's got to peak somewhere," he said, "but it doesn't. They say Pat O'Dea of Wisconsin drop kicked a 62-yarder against Northwestern. Same distance as Gipp." Spyder leaned sideways, away from me, but his eyes stayed fastened on me. "I guess it's got to be true. With Gipp, you figure it's one more piece of the legend, but who's going to make something up like that about some forgotten guy from Wisconsin?"

"I guess I could believe it."

"You think they got it right?"

"About O'Shea?"

"O'Dea. 'The Kangaroo Kicker.' It was a lifetime ago, 1898." Spyder was frowning. "I mean, did they get the distance right? Maybe it was 55 yards. Maybe it was 65."

"Does it matter all that much? It's a helluva long kick, either way."

Spyder stood up and backed away a few steps and chewed at his lip. "Maybe to Jack Pence. He had a 59-yarder. Maybe he wanted to say that no one drop kicked a ball farther than him. No TV cameras back then, probably no photographs. Think they had nice, neat lines painted on the field so you could gauge distances? Or maybe they played on an open field with the only markers at the goal line. Hard to measure things."

I shrugged and nodded. Spyder leaned forward to spit gently, then looked up and arched his eyebrows. "Maybe it never even happened," he said. "Maybe it was really a punt. Maybe some sportswriter just wrote it that way. You believe it?"

Spyder stood up and walked down a few steps, then turned to face me. He leaned in with one hand on his knee and lowered his voice.

"You know what Jim Thorpe used to do after he turned pro? Before the game, he would stand at the 50-yard line and drop kick the ball through one set of goal posts. Then he would turn around and drop kick the ball through the goal posts at the other end." Spyder grinned and raised himself up. "Think about it. Can you imagine the look on the other team's faces? You see a guy do that, don't you kind of wonder what else he's capable of doing?"

Spyder arched his back as he stretched his arms and looked up at the washed-out sky, with just a sheen of blue. Two dozen Canadian geese were flying southeast in a neat V, honking away, with one bird by itself, off to the side, out of a spot, but keeping pace. I wondered whether a bird always knows where it's going once it sets out, where its final destination is, how to know when to stop. All I knew at that moment is that I had never heard of Pat O'Dea. I had seen pictures of Jim Thorpe, with facial features that looked like they were hammered out of stone, and eyes that looked like they were forever squinting into the sun. He looked like a guy who could drop kick a football 50 yards. I think Spyder Pollett looked like the same kind of guy.

I turned to Spyder, frowning. "So, did these guys go to the pros then? Did they drop kick there?"

Spyder folded his arms and shook his head rapidly. "That was a different time. Not like today. It might have been 'Dutch' Clark had the last drop kick in the pros. For the Lions, 1937. He made the NFL Hall of Fame, but not for being a kicker."

Spyder leaned over the railing, watching students below file past on the sidewalk. They looked neat and orderly, the way a marching band does before they all fan out in different directions. "Yeah, all those guys are forgotten," Spyder said. "They could do things hardly anyone else could do, but who cares now? What good would all that talent do them today? Where do you put it? Just all go to waste, all be forgotten."

I shifted my weight back and forth, rolling my shoulders as I felt a tiny shiver. It was past five o'clock, still early enough in spring that it got cool by late afternoon in the shade. Students were beginning an exodus from the library. "Well," I said, "you sure remember them."

"Yeah, I'll be the only one pretty soon, I expect." He laughed softly, then wheeled around to face me with a big grin, wagging a finger at me.

"Hey, Mr. English Major, I'll bet you didn't know this. Way back, there were six brothers, blood relations of Edgar Allan Poe himself, and they all played football for Princeton. All six, right? Now, one of them, Arthur, becomes an All-American. One year he beats Yale with a 90-yard touchdown run. Next year, get this: he drop kicks the game-winning field goal to beat Yale. Again."

Spyder reached into his pocket for his wallet, slipping in two fingers to pluck out a folded piece of lined notebook paper. He wiggled the paper at me, then opened it and began to read. "'For an instant Poe gauged the distance to and direction of the goal posts. He dropped the ball carefully, caught it squarely on the toe of that good right foot of his, raised it in the air in a graceful curve, and the crowd held its breath as it sailed until the spheroid stopped its upward flight. Then it moved gracefully toward the ground, and a great shout went up from the Princeton stand. The ball had gone directly between the goal posts.'"

Spyder arched his back and laughed, then turned the paper around to show me the handwriting. "From the newspaper," he said. "I copied it down because I wanted it exactly right." Spyder folded the scrap of paper but kept it in his hands and smiled. "That's the kind of historic writing you do someday, I bet."

Spyder coughed gently and cleared his throat. "There's something else," he said. "One more thing. That was the first time Arthur Poe ever tried a drop kick. Imagine that? And he only got the chance because the regular kicker was injured." He opened the paper again and glanced at it, then quickly folded it back up. "Some epitaph, huh? You wonder why they gave him a chance." Spyder pulled out his wallet and tucked the paper back inside.

I clutched my books tighter as I stood up to leave, then stopped. "Hey, Spyder? I was just wondering. What's it like to kick a game-winning field goal? What's that feel like, to feel like Arthur Poe?"

I wasn't sure if he was going to answer. He stuck his hands in both pockets and looked past me, toward the entrance to the library. I heard students laughing as they came out the thick wooden door, and it creaked and banged twice before it shut.

I saw Spyder's chest swell softly. He scrunched his face and shielded his eyes with one hand as he looked off toward the sun. "You've got to keep your head down," he said, "so you really can't tell if you're on-target. It's like watching a film, sort of in slow motion, and the crowd is a couple frames ahead of you. So you find the ball in mid-flight, wondering if it will be long enough, whether it will veer off to either side. You feel frozen, and you feel helpless. Here you are—you have the ability to do something almost no one else can—and you're not going to get any credit at all by only coming close. There are just so many things that can go wrong. Everybody seems to know before you do that it's good, and then everything around you explodes."

Spyder turned his gaze to me and ran his teeth gently over his lower lip. "You'd think you'd feel this exhilaration, this joy, and I guess some do. But it's not necessarily like that. You just feel relief. You're glad it's over."

I wouldn't say that Spyder Pollett had a lot of close friends. I think he counted me as one of his better friends, but that wasn't saying much. I liked talking with him. He seemed genuine and kindhearted, and I never saw him angry. He put me at ease, but I know some people didn't always feel comfortable around him. I didn't think you could blame them for getting that feeling. But there was one more thing I needed to ask him, even if I thought I was trespassing on a secret, like asking for the secret ingredient in a recipe, and I didn't know if I would get another chance.

"Hey. Hey, Spyder? I was just wondering. How does a guy drop a pointy football so that it bounces straight off the ground, then time it perfectly so that you kick it at the perfect moment? I mean, it sort of defies logic, doesn't it?"

Spyder's face was bowed, so I couldn't tell if he was grinning or just thinking about an answer. But I didn't mind waiting. "It's not strength. It's not power," he said without raising his head. Then he looked up. "I suppose there are laws of physics you can use to calculate kicking or punting a football—like air drag, launch speed, stuff like that—if you want to. But what really counts is touch, having a feel for it. Make sense? Ever do any trapshooting? There's this point in the sky, see, where you anticipate the target is going to fly through, and you're connecting the flight of the bullet with the flight of the clay target, in an instant. There's that point—that spot where it all connects—and all the rest of it is just empty space."

Spyder rolled his neck from side to side, then lazily windmilled his arms. "And I imagine," he said, turning to go, "that if you can drop kick a football 62 yards, you're not too worried about all the empty space in the sky."

I never did see Spyder drop kick a football. But Bruno did. He was out early one Sunday morning in late May, passing the stadium, and he saw a lone figure on the field. He knew it couldn't be anyone else.

"You know, he wasn't really kicking much," Bruno said. "Mostly he would pace off three steps, then drop the ball. Not even kick it, just practice dropping it, and lowering his foot to meet the ball. Over and over. Finally, he kicked it."

"How far?" I asked. "Far, real far, like 40, 50 yards?"

Bruno pursed his lips and twisted his torso. "Nah, not that far. But, you know, I don't think he was trying to kick it hard. Or far. He didn't even look up at the ball after he kicked it. He kept his head down all the time. It didn't seem to even matter to him where the ball was going. Or maybe he just knew. Somehow, he just knew."

"Now, you saw him kick back in high school, right?" I asked.

"Yeah, sure. He was good, he was real good. I think he had some kind of school record for consecutive field goals."

"But he didn't drop kick back then, of course? What was he, a soccer-style kicker? Most all of them are nowadays."

"Nope, he was one of those old-fashioned style kickers—straight-ahead. He was the only one I remember who did that." Bruno chuckled. "Ever see those old-time photos of those kickers, their arms stuck out shoulder-high, like they think if they flap them hard enough, they can take off like a bird?"

"I guess. So, how'd he come to this drop kicking?"

Bruno cocked his head. "Don't know. I really don't. But to practice whenever you wanted, you'd have to find a guy to hold the ball for you, another to snap it to the holder. Maybe he figured doing it alone was the only way he could do it."

That fall, months after graduation, I came back to campus for a football game. The sun throbbed with warmth, and the leaves on the trees gurgled with the rush of wind. I was visiting with friends in the parking lot, drinking coffee and eating sandwiches, wondering if Spyder would show. I was also wondering if this would be the year he was going to graduate.

Fifteen minutes before kickoff, I saw Spyder loping toward us, hands in his jacket pockets, shoulders swaying, a smile just visible under his bowed head. "I was afraid I'd miss you," I said, sticking my hand out to shake his.

"You know me," he said. "Just couldn't break away from the library."

"Right," I said, pointing to his hands. "Guess you forgot your books."

Spyder turned his palms up and tilted his head to the side. "They'll be waiting for me. So. What are you up to now?"

"Teaching English in high school. What a surprise, huh?"

"No apologies necessary." Spyder nodded, and I thought he looked happy to hear the news. "It's good to find your niche," he said softly. "And one day you'll be a professor, come back here to ennoble future generations."

I smiled. "Sure. Sure, I'll do some ennobling down the line."

I hesitated. I wanted to ask Spyder something else. Instead, we just followed the crowd into the stadium. It was a perfect day for a college football game. There was everything to enjoy in those moments, but I soon grew restless, like late October weather. I wondered already if I'd ever get back again, and I wondered whether I could dare excuse myself early, like Spyder used to do.

I started thinking about other games I had seen during my college years, but I couldn't remember victories or defeats that well, or who was with us as we watched. Instead, for some reason I thought of Jim Thorpe and his kicking exhibitions. And I realized I was mistaken. I didn't know what a guy looked like who could drop kick a football 50 yards. I was trying to picture Spyder in a woolen football jersey and those baggy old-time pants that hung as shapelessly as canvas over an easel, and it wasn't hard to do. And I could see him, too, inside a lighthouse, his face pressed close to a windowpane being hammered with rain and hail and slammed with gusts of damning wind, Spyder staring out onto a lake where a ship fought waves that threatened to gulp it down whole.

But mostly I liked to imagine Spyder Pollett on a green field, standing off alone, mindless of a screaming crowd, fans frantically beating their arms like birds trapped in an attic. Spyder wearing a leather helmet, and a fat, weathered ball falling like a single tear from between those steady hands, held before him as if he were an ancient, primitive priest about to deliver a sacrifice. And then he swings his leg, and the crowd, as one, holds its breath as the spheroid takes flight.

Good Hands

Tamara Adelman

I work at a no-frills kind of place, where I like to hang out with the manager, Liz, when I'm between appointments. She says she's never seen a massage therapist with so many clients who buy packages—which means I have a lot of repeats. Liz's brown hair is always shiny, and there has been only one day in three years that I've seen her without makeup. Her voice is kind, and when she was just a little girl—her mother told me—she'd organize all the children on the playground—had them standing in lines.

My mom would be hard-pressed to remember anything positive about me as a kid, even though I was a good kid and still never forget her birthday. It was Friday.

"Hi, Mom, I'm calling to say happy birthday."

"Thanks for remembering," she said, and then asked me how some ex-boyfriend from my distant past was doing, and if my long-estranged (from her) brother and his family—whom she has never met—got swept away by some rains on the East Coast.

"Okay, time to hang up," she said after about five minutes of uncomfortable conversation, none of it about how I was doing.

I have heard that people who are drawn to healing have something to heal in themselves. This intrigued me. I'd always felt a part of me was broken. I grew up lost, had a hard time feeling connected to people, and, according to my mother, wasn't exceptionally good at anything. I drifted as the stray tend to do, from place to place, passion to passion. After quitting an MBA program, I enrolled in massage school, where I learned a new language—the language of touch.

Massage therapy seemed like underachieving, except that the bar was set pretty low on achieving, so there was no going under it. My mother warned that I'd ruin my hands, so I had to seriously consider that.

Once I started touching people, I didn't want to stop. It was like Braille to a blind person—I discovered the path to wholeness resided in my fingertips. Finally, I felt connected, like the broken part had found a fix.

I witnessed a stilling of myself when I was in the treatment room. I was able to control everything: the temperature, the lighting, and even telling the client when to turn over.

The room was like a womb for me: dark, with soothing music, a candle. There were times in the beginning when I still heard the words, *I miss my mother.*

Sometimes I got a little teary.

I spent eighth grade in a boarding school and was homesick the whole year. I'd never been away from home, but after my parents' divorce I learned that a building didn't constitute a home anyway. Once my dad got remarried and moved away with my little brother, and my mom went off the deep end, I was on my own.

I missed everybody all the time.

For high school, I went back with my mom, who decided to move to Florida three days before school started. She'd always wanted to move there; it said so in her high school yearbook.

"I thank the Course in Miracles for giving me the support to make this move," she declared during the drive from Wisconsin, while I sat right next to her, worried I would miss the first day of school.

"I've got a brother who's an alcoholic and a crook. Can you imagine, stealing from your own mother's estate? That's exactly what Jack did. And my father, who told me 'Judy, go jump in the lake,' me— the only one who has any sense—let him get away with it!" She took the cleansing breath she'd learned to quit smoking.

"My brother killed my mother!" she concluded. "She may have had a stroke and emphysema, but she died of a broken heart!"

What a crap-head, I would never do that to you, I thought, but couldn't say.

"If I hadn't married your father—the most indecent man I have ever known—I would have been at my mother's bedside. But no, your Grandpa Ollie told me 'Don't worry, dear, we'll take care of you. Your place is with your husband—in Israel. We're your family now.' Well, a lot of good that did me!"

I counted the telephone poles through Georgia.

"My mother couldn't even talk, she had paralysis!"

I knew the feeling.

"The way you're looking at me, that glare, it's really unbecoming. But go ahead, you're a teenager, I'm not gonna take it personally."

"This drive is really boring," I said.

"I just want you to realize that without the Course in Miracles, I'd be dead!"

"I wish I knew where we were going to live," and I wished I had some friends in Florida.

"You're such a planner! Could you give it a rest for a minute?" Her tone implied this was like some kind of birth defect.

"When you were a little girl, I couldn't leave you in a room alone for five minutes without you screaming. It was really hard for me to get a break. You always had to be entertained."

I smirked.

"You think you know everything. Well, I have news for you," she breathed out, heavy on the exhale.

I braced myself.

"Someday you'll understand. Someday, when your life has not turned out as you had planned, someday when you have children of your own—children who do not appreciate you, having to plan everything around them—when you have a son who doesn't send you a birthday card, someday when I am dead—I hope you can understand what it was like for me to have no support!" She banged her hand on the steering wheel for emphasis.

By the time we got to Florida I was exhausted.

My mom was a cat that wanted to be petted one minute, then would bite you the next.

It was an impossible job, being her kid. Even though I was a hard worker, my resignation has finally been left at her desk. I am still trying to separate all the places where I stop and she starts, but my new work helps me do that.

Now, in my job, people are happy to see me. Soothing a tight neck, helping a sore back or leg, and ending a headache makes me feel powerful. New clients are always surprised when I walk into the room after they've gotten situated on the table and I am able to touch exactly the spot that causes them pain.

People always ask me, "Isn't being a masseuse hard work? I mean, don't your hands get tired?"

"Not really," I say. "It doesn't feel like work to me."

Because, where I work, all the cats like being petted.

Staircase

Deborah George

There is this one thing Keats had said
but she couldn't think of it

or one cornucopia of goodness
to spread on top of the frozen butter.

Nothing could delay the curfew,
or cure the wounds too fresh to scab over

mothers shouting at children from an iron staircase
Do not swallow crocheted doilies, sheet music stamped by Mozart,

or the Tappan Range in the kitchen, you might hurt yourself!
The cupboard flies open—visions float from the shelf cradling

Grannie Hazel's nicked bowl, Aunt Betty's turkey platter
with the fall scene of a Bavarian woodchopper,

ax slung over his shoulders, logs stacked
in his carriage like Tootsie Rolls,

the wonder if he'd make it home before snow fell,
before dark. She ate a banana for dinner,

curried chicken for lunch,
swallowed a Spanish latte

with crushed almond milk
in the afternoon. She walked

the aisles of a food market,
purchased food like a man

wanted to break commandments,
heard the preacher's spitty whisper

Thou shalt not kill the man
who attacked thine daughter,

your first born, the one who liked to climb the most fragile limbs
of magnolia trees all the way to the top, afraid of nothing.

Pitchblende

Jessica Cuello

I measured the lives
I loved, the way I tested

elements until I was sore,
numb in the wrists:

Pierre's francs per day,
how many gooseberries

for six jars of jam, how hot
the stove, the first time

Irene laughed, the age
she was afraid of strangers.

My first week back from birth
I ran from the lab in panic

to see if our baby was there.
Theory is fine.

But I couldn't slave
for it. I preferred to stir

a thousand times, increase
the flame, and stir again.

I preferred to go after
the thing itself, to hold

it in my hand: a salt:
a color and a weight

arrayed. I knew there was,
inside the pitchblende,

an energy that did not depend
on sunlight, heat, or cold.

Paranormal

Our first bike trip together,
I didn't turn around.
I loosened my shirt,

smelled my own body
on the path. Even
the fleshy berries

made me aware your eyes
were on my back. Before that,
before the honeymoon,

before I agreed to live
in France—a tug in the air.
The letter I did not answer—

my silence—vibrated
between our countries.
In the Carpathians,

I glanced at a map.
The paper was textured
and raised across your province

—the spot of color glowed.
In the courtyard of the Sorbonne,
I felt a wave. Turning,

I saw you had passed.
Even in the dark
you found me.

Pierre Curie believed in paranormal phenomena and used to attend séances. He believed that he saw objects moving across the room and that there was, in his opinion, "a whole domain of entirely new facts and physical states in space of which we have no conception."

Markings

Teresa Milbrodt

Breakfast with my sister is a disaster. She wants to make muffins, but I have to crack the eggs and measure spices and hold the bowl while she stirs. She can only use her right hand since the stroke, and the work I can do versus the work she can do leaves her frowning. I'm wearing a short sleeved shirt so my tattoos show, which further annoys her. She doesn't like being reminded of them. When my sister spreads jam on her muffin, the knife slips and falls onto her white pants. I help her change. She grumps around afterwards, but there's not much either of us can do.

I need to get out of the house and suggest a walk to the park. My sister slumps on the couch and crosses her arms.

"Once you get outside you'll feel better," I say as I sit beside her and ready her socks and shoes. "Now give me your foot."

She refuses to move, so I bend down and grab her ankle and rest it on my lap. I tug her sock over her toes, then slide on her shoe. She knows my fingers ache in the morning, but she's decided that if I'm going to torture her, she's going to torture me back.

"I'm not trying to upset you," I say, though she'd accuse me of that if she could talk. I can see it in her eyes and hear it in the voice she used to have.

"I know what you're saying, so you don't have to look at me so loudly," I say as I pull the second sock over her foot.

My sister grimaces. She thinks I'm making fun, but I'm being honest. All her gestures come with words. Sometimes we talk through raised eyebrows, finger-points, and nods.

I think about saying something to her about assisted living facilities. There's a nice one on the other end of town. I called them yesterday to inquire about rates, but I don't want her to accuse me of making threats. In the past week, putting my sister in an assisted living facility has become more of a serious consideration. I hate to say that I'm getting too old for this, but I am.

Once her feet have been properly attired, I drag my sister out the door to the park.

"The sun will do us both good," I say.

My sister glances back and forth as we walk the two blocks. She doesn't like being with me in public places because of my short-sleeved shirts and short skirts.

"Really," I mutter. "What good are these lovely pictures if they're hidden?"

On my right arm is Aphrodite. There's a snake curling around my left arm, ending on an apple at my wrist. A female angel wields a sword on my right leg, and on my left leg, Eve demurely covers her intimate areas with her hands. I like that my tattoos have been distorted by cellulite—Eve and the angel have gained weight and wrinkled along with me. They are meant to be seen. I am meant to be seen. And I am old enough not to care what other people think.

At the park, my sister eases down on a bench. It's been a year since her stroke. When she was released from the hospital I moved in to care for her. She didn't want to go to a facility. *Too expensive*, she wrote on the pad of paper that had become her mouth. She wanted to stay in her apartment. But I know that all day long she thinks intelligent things that she can't say. It drives her crazy. She was a teacher after all; she's used to giving instructions and being obeyed.

While I am sympathetic, I get frustrated with her moods. If she had an assisted living apartment, she'd have her own bed, her own space, and wear a little alert device with a button she could press if she needed help. The nurses and other residents would probably be more patient with her than me. But my sister doesn't want to move. The process is more complicated since she has her wits about her. It's easier to put family members in a home when they don't know what's going on.

A fat woman puffing by on a morning jog stares at us. I smile and wave. My sister glances over to me and bites her lip.

When we were children, we lived above our mother's tattoo shop. Mother wore skirts that covered her ankles and blouses with sleeves to the wrist, but everyone in town knew that her skin, save her hands and feet and face, sang with color. Mother tattooed soldiers from a nearby military base during the day, but at night women came wrapped in shawls and darkness. They wanted roses on the small of their backs, said their husbands found the markings erotic.

When we walked to the bank or grocery store my sister strode several paces ahead of us, pretending she wasn't related. Later, when she was in high school, we couldn't get her to accompany us on any outing. She said she had to stay home to study. Even then she was planning her escape. Mother must have known. But she also knew we were always being watched. That was why she walked with the light grace of a dancer, and made sure my sister and I were angels in public. If we acted out she'd spank us so hard we couldn't sit down all evening.

In the tattoo shop I sat beside Mother as she drew designs on arms and legs and backs with a template. She stretched the skin tight and switched on the tattooing machine, sponged away ink and blood as she worked. My sister curled herself tight as a cat in a living room chair and shut out the din of the tattoo needle. She went to college. I studied tattooing with Mother. She started inking my skin when I was fifteen, and I continued working on myself when I was old enough to learn the art.

After she'd moved out of Mother's apartment, my sister turned and walked in the other direction when she saw Mother and me on the street. Mother was demure, didn't say anything about my sister's rebuffs, but at home while listening to her usual radio programs, she kept a handkerchief at the ready. I hated to see her mourn the person my sister had become, but she'd always worried about appearances.

"They're not staring at you," I whisper to her in the park.

My sister looks normally old. There's nothing odd about her at first glance, though she spends long minutes in front of the bathroom mirror, turning her head this way and that, trying to push wrinkles off her face with her good hand. Sitting beside me makes her even less conspicuous. She doesn't believe me when I say this, and slides to the other side of the bench. I shrug and chat with passers-by, particularly the older gentlemen. Wilson pauses to say hello.

"You're looking fresh as spring daisies," he says to us.

I thank him. My sister looks away.

Wilson and I talk about his dog and his grandchildren and the pleasant weather.

"We need to get coffee together," he says. "Make a date of it."

I say that would be lovely. My sister hunches lower on the bench. Wilson tips his ball cap and wishes us both a good day.

"Who else is going to flirt with old men except for waitresses who want bigger tips?" I mutter to my sister after Wilson leaves. "They deserve a good flirt with no strings attached."

My sister never believed in flirting. When she could talk, she said it was disingenuous.

"I'm not going to bring someone home," I say. "We're just playing."

My sister sighs and crosses her good arm over the limp one. She once dated a man for two years before she discovered he was married, so she's very concerned about who's genuine and who's not. While I understand that, I won't deny myself an enjoyable experience because of silly fears. I've had men friends, shared a bed with a few of them, and wouldn't mind doing it again, but my sister would never agree to such a thing in our apartment. I try to be considerate of her needs, though she doesn't appreciate how my life changed when I moved in with her. No more boyfriends. No more nights with guests. No more casual chatter over meals.

My sister glances from side to side and then down at her stomach.

"What's the matter?" I say. I have learned to be keen to her movements. "Hungry? You didn't have much breakfast."

She glances sideways at me, shrugs.

"I'll get us some ice cream," I say as I stand and stretch.

As I walk to a vendor, the tattooed snake twists lazily around my arm and Eve's hips jiggle. I love my whole body except for my hands. They're wrinkled and knobbed and never stop aching. Sometimes I want to be a starfish, chop off my fingers and grow new ones. I forgot to take my pain medication after the muffin debacle because my sister was weeping.

When I come back with the ice cream cones, my sister holds out her good hand but looks nervous, like she wishes she hadn't admitted she was hungry. She has a hard time keeping up with ice cream drips, gets one down the front of her lavender blouse and starts sniffling.

"Don't worry," I say, daubing her with a napkin and tucking another one into her collar.

She cringes, hates bibs, but it's the best way to catch the ice cream drips. I eat my ice cream and enjoy the sun for a few minutes.

My sister tugs on my arm. She's dropped her ice cream on the sidewalk (intentionally) and wants to leave.

"Honey," I say, "we cleaned the ice cream off your blouse."

She tugs my arm again.

"We haven't even been here twenty minutes," I say. "I'm not ready to leave. Relax. Close your eyes. Breathe the air. Feel the sun."

She whimpers, stands up, and pulls my arm again. She wants to say how embarrassed she is. I wrest free of her grasp and stand beside her.

"Sit," I say and push down on her shoulder. She never wants to be in the park very long. It's irritating. "I'm sick of making allowances for you. For once we're going to stay when I want to."

My sister pouts. She's gotten very good at that in the past year. In desperate moments I wish she'd have another stroke. It wouldn't be a great shame if she lost her capacity for pride. Being old embarrasses her. Old people embarrass her.

I finish my ice cream. My sister is stone still. Fuming. I don't want to treat her like she's seven, but she acts that age when she doesn't get her way. I resent that she resents me. It's not easy to care for someone who does not want care. I worry that if I put her in assisted living she'll despise me, but if I don't put her in assisted living we'll hate each other even more.

"I'm sorry I got mad at you," I say.

She stares at her right arm, the lifeless one.

I sigh but notice Stuart doing the daily crossword and glancing at us from two benches over. We see often him at the park in the morning. He lives in the retirement complex nearby. He's a kind man, sometimes brings us coffee or a pastry from the bakery. We have shared details. I know his wife had a stroke five years ago and died of a second stroke two years ago. He knows I operated my mother's tattoo shop for decades, but sold it seven years ago.

"Sorry," says Stuart when he sees me looking at him. "I didn't mean to interrupt."

I make room for Stuart on the bench and wave him over. At the moment, I'd like the company of someone who isn't my sister. Someone who isn't terribly cross. Someone who, and I'm ashamed to admit this, can talk.

My sister stiffens, grabs my arm with her good hand, and tries to pull me away from Stuart like I'm three years old. Sometimes we fight over who gets to gets to protect who.

"You look nice today," says Stuart to my sister.

My sister tries to smile. She hates being singled out as much as she hates my flirting. I think she sees the same coquette in me that she saw in Mother, who tended to flirt with her unmarried male clients. I don't pretend to know what happened in Mother's bedroom after we were asleep, but I don't doubt she had company from time to time. I see nothing wrong with that, since I've done likewise.

My sister usually hated my mother in silences, but there was one time they argued at dinner and my sister yelled, "You don't even know who our father is."

Mother set down her fork and blotted her lips with a napkin.

"Do you want his address?" she said quietly.

"You have it?" my sister squeaked.

Mother nodded.

"Why didn't you tell us?" my sister said.

"You never asked," said Mother.

"I want it," said my sister. "Of course I want it."

I watched Mother copy words from a small leather-bound book onto a piece of paper. A name and a street address, I imagine. Possibly someone in town. Mother had impeccable handwriting. She could have been a calligrapher.

My sister folded the paper and slipped it in her pocket. Mother asked if I wanted the address, too. I said I'd think about it, but knew my answer would be no. If this man was too embarrassed to visit us, why should I care about him? I imagined he might be watching Mother and my sister and me from street corners, monitoring our progress to the grocery store, but I assumed he had his own wife and children and was less ashamed of them.

I never asked my sister if she spoke with the man, but she wanted the paper and the opportunity. I doubt her pride would have let her chat with our father and divulge what she knew. There are many questions I keep silent when I'm around her.

I help Stuart with the crossword, correct a couple answers that don't fit the grid. We chat about my mother's tattoo shop. He says he'd like to see it someday, and perhaps take us out to lunch afterwards. I nod and say that would be fun. I don't tell him that sometimes I find it difficult to visit the storefront, but that's because I can't work a needle like I used to.

"You should see this," says Stuart. He begins to unbutton his shirt, showing off his wrinkled chest. My sister puts her hand over her mouth, but Stuart keeps unbuttoning until he can slide the fabric off his shoulders and reveal the tattoo of a falcon on his arm and one of a raven on his back. Their wings droop, preparing to land on some invisible perch. I appreciate the pictures as well as the other marks on Stuart's body, patches of light and dark and scarred skin. After a certain age everyone is a novel.

Stuart buttons his shirt and we resume chatting about how it's nearly lunchtime. He asks if we would like to join him for a sandwich. Our hands inch closer on the bench. When our fingers graze, I feel a little surge in my chest. Surprising, almost, how the sensation doesn't change. Stuart cradles my hand in his and rubs his thumb over my fingers.

My sister screams.

Stuart and I stare at her.

"What on earth is the matter?" I say. "Why can't you have a pleasant morning at the park like a normal person?"

"Is she right in the head?" Stuart whispers.

"I don't know," I say, not caring that my sister can hear me. "Goodness knows what's working in her mind and what isn't."

That shuts my sister up. She gives me a good stare, stands up, and starts walking out of the park. Stuart and I watch her for a moment.

"Should she leave on her own?" he says.

"No," I sigh. "I need to go after her."

"It was pleasant chatting with you," he says, squeezing my hand. His touch makes my fingers hurt, but I don't care. I catch up with my sister at the stoplight.

"You are perfectly awful," I yell.

She grins at me, malicious, then begins to cross when the light changes. I almost don't go after her, but Mother would never forgive me. As I trail my sister, I remember how, when we were little and played games of pretend, she was the good fairy and made me be the evil one. She got to decide because she was older, but I liked my role more than she wanted me to.

In the middle of the street I grab my sister's fingers and try to pull her back, but she yanks her hand from my grasp. We reach the sidewalk and I take her hand again. She screams like I was trying to kidnap her. Passers-by stare. She keeps screaming. I know they are not looking at me or the pictures on my body. They're thinking *Batty old woman.* I ache for my sister and her wordlessness. Family should care for family. That's what Mother said. That's why I cared for Mother until she was on so many medications that neither of us could keep them straight and she needed to go into a home.

I let go of my sister's hand, turn around, and walk back to the curb. Stuart should still be at the park. I'll explain everything to him. He'll understand. We can go for lunch together. My sister can unlock the apartment door with her good hand. She could live alone, in her own small place, if there were nurses close by to assist her. I have known this for a while. I almost peer over my shoulder to see if she changed her mind and is following me back to the park, but I don't care to look.

Three Fire Signs

Eleanore Lee

1. Hearth

Hold on to the memory:
I hold my hands to the fire, light through my fingers.
Kittens and puppies and strangers press close too.
Your flickering makes long shadows in my room.
A dependable source of energy, renewable resource.
I stay where the heat is.
I curl beside you in the night.

2. Forest

It's been a long, dry season.
"Too late to stop her now," say the old-timers.
Touch a match to me now and I'll explode in flames,
Roar down southern slopes, singe baby animals
In my path.
Smell me in the hot wind,
Black desolation after and a memory of
The heat.
God knows, I've raked through ashes before.

3.   House

"Fire?" I whisper.

"What is it now?" you say, standing in the door. "I've
given all I can."

Together in the haze of smoke,

Smoke curling out the windows, seeping under doors.

Did you notice the radiator cord was frayed?

Whole houses can go in a minute, I've seen it happen.

Glow in upstairs window now.

It wasn't a palace, but it kept out the rain.

Contributors

Tamara Adelman is a massage therapist, triathlete, and freelance writer living in Santa Monica, California. She has competed in seven Ironman races, and is currently enrolled in the Creative Nonfiction Certificate Program at UCLA. She can be found most days looking out at the Santa Monica Bay, as she writes the next story or trains for the next race—in passionate pursuit of perfection: the finish line.

Dorthea Balabus began life in Long Island, New York, enjoying the ocean and lakes that surrounded a simple, smalltown life. She married her high school boyfriend. Two delightful daughters later this little family moved to Southern California. She and her family took a cross-country train trip in 1963 to visit the New York World's Fair; *Eastward Ho* is a peek into their memorable trip. In 2009, Dorthea retired from a Human Resources career to enjoy the roles of Grand and Great-Grandma in beautiful Oregon.

Daneen Bergland's poems have appeared in numerous journals, most recently in *Poet Lore*, *Cerise Press*, *Propeller Magazine*, *The Burnside Review*, and *Verse Daily*. In 2009 she received a fellowship from Oregon Literary Arts. She teaches in the University Studies department at Portland State University.

Drawing inspiration from a range of psychological landscapes, **Paula Marafino Bernett's** work reflects a deep curiosity about the mind's cognitive forays into language and association, not constrained by linear thought. Her poems have appeared or are forthcoming in *Anemone Sidecar*, *California Quarterly (CQ)*, *The Chaffin Journal*, *Eclipse*, *The Hiss Quarterly*, *Margie*, *Milk Money*, *Rattle*, *Salamander*, *Sierra Nevada College Review*, and *Tar River Poetry*. Paula holds an MFA from Sarah Lawrence College and makes her home in Taos, NM.

Rob E. Boley earned both his BA and MA degrees in English from Wright State University. His fiction has also found a home in *Necrotic Tissue*, *Macabre Cadaver*, the *Day Terrors* anthology, and *A capella Zoo*. He is currently working on a novel. Meet him online at www.facebook.com/rob.boley.

Wanda Lea Brayton is a former college librarian and construction news reporter, and has been writing poetry since 1973. Her poems have been accepted by *The Pedestal Magazine*, *Oak Bend Review*, *Main Street Rag*, and *Clackamas Literary Review* (2010). She was the featured poet in March 2011 on the World Poetry site, and various poems have been read on the World Poetry Cafe Radio station in Vancouver, as well as placed on display there (including at the Pablo Neruda celebration), and another poem was further exhibited at the John Lennon Peace Tower in Iceland.

Kevin Breen is a fiction writer from Grand Rapids, Michigan, whose stories have appeared in about twenty journals, including most recently *Bayou Magazine*, *Other Voices*, *Natural Bridge*, and *Orchid*. In addition to more stories, he's working on a novel about a serial rapist based on real events from his home town.

H. D. Brown lives and works on the bank of Chico Creek in California, in a house full of poems, books, guitars, home-made guitars, home-made wine, and projects in various stages of completion. He has recent and forthcoming work in *Poetry Quarterly, Hawk and Whippoorwill, Muscle and Blood*, and other literary journals. He is also an associate professor of American Literature and Culture at California State University Chico.

Charles Cantrell is a semi-retired English professor. His poems have appeared in many journals and anthologies, most recently *ABZ, The Hurriane Review, Chiron Review, Poem*, and *Stoneboat*. Other works are forthcoming in *Green Hills Literary Lantern, The South Carolina Review Paterson Literary Review, Connecticut River Review*, and *Clackamas Literary Review*. He has been nominated twice for a Pushcart Prize.

Author **Talia Carner's** heart-wrenching suspense novels, *Puppet Child* and *China Doll*, were hailed for exposing society's ills. Her next novel, *Jerusalem Maiden*, depicting a woman's struggle for self-expression against her society's religious dictates, will be published by Harper-Collins in June 2011. Carner's award-winning short stories and essays have appeared in numerous anthologies and literary publications. Please check www.TaliaCarner.com.

Paul Crenshaw's stories and essays have appeared or are forthcoming in *Best American Essays 2005* and *2011, Shenandoah, North American Review, Southern Humanities Review, Hayden's Ferry Review*, and *South Dakota Review*, among others. He teaches writing and literature at Elon University.

Jessica Cuello is a graduate of Barnard College who teaches French in Central NY. Her poems have appeared in *Copper Nickel*, *RHINO*, *Conte*, *Tampa Review*, and other journals. In 2010, she received two "Best of the Net" nominations and the Vivienne Haigh-Wood Poetry Prize. A chapbook of poems about Marie Curie is forthcoming from Kattywompus Press in 2011. Her first full-length manuscript was a finalist for the Bull City Press 2010 First Book Prize.

Rudy Dicks has been a reporter, copy editor, sports editor, and managing editor for daily newspapers in Ohio, New Jersey, and New York City. As a sportswriter, he covered football, baseball, basketball, boxing, and track and field, from high school to the pros. A native of Ohio, Dicks graduated from Oberlin College with a degree in English. He successfully made the lone point-after he tried during his high school football career, but he never attempted a drop kick in a game.

Jack Donahue has published numerous short stories and poems in literary and arts journals such as *Eugene O'Neill Review*, *Confrontation*, *Crucible*, *The Mediterranean Review*, *Folio* and others throughout the U.S. and Europe. A number of Jack's plays have been produced at the Bailiwick Theatre Company, Chicago, IL, Northport Arts Coalition, Northport, NY, Arena Repertory Theatre, Farmingdale, NY, among many others.. Aside from his devotion to writing, Jack is an ordained minister currently serving as Pastor of a RCA church in Bayside, New York.

KC Eib holds a BA in Theatre from Missouri State University and an MFA in Creative Writing from the University of Alaska—Fairbanks. He has written, produced, and directed performances through Kansas

City's Just Off Broadway, The Alcott Arts Center, and The KC Fringe Festival among others. His nonfiction publications can be found in *Alaska Quarterly Review* and *Fourteen Hills*. *CLR* marks his first poetry publication. He currently resides in Bremerton, WA.

Greg Evason writes poems, short stories, essays, plays, and novels. He also draws, collages, paints, plays the piano, and takes photos when so moved. So far, many of his poems and a handful of short stories, drawings, collages, and photographs have appeared in numerous magazines both on and off line.

A former career diplomat, **Lawrence Farrar** served in Japan (five times), Norway, Germany, and Washington, DC. A Dartmouth graduate, he holds a Stanford MA in Japanese history, studied at the Inter-University Center in Tokyo, and graduated from the National Defense University. His stories have appeared in *Red Cedar Review*, *The Mac-Guffin*, *Red Wheelbarrow*, *The G.W. Review*, *Colere*, *Green Hills Literary Lantern* (currently online), *The Worcester Review*, *New Plains Review*, and *Straylight*. Another piece is slated for the *Evening Street Review*. Farrar has completed two draft novels, both set in Japan. He and his wife, Keiko, live in North Oaks, Minnesota.

Kristi Garboushian holds an MFA in Creative Writing from Arizona State University. Her work has appeared in numerous publications, including the *Cimarron Review*, *Safundi: The Journal of South African and American Comparative Studies*, *Blackbird*, and the collection *American War Poetry: An Anthology*. She resides in Chandler, Arizona, and works as a community college secretary.

Deborah George was named as a finalist in the 2010 Beyond Baroque Poetry Contest. She co-authored *Ignatius Rising: The Life of John Kennedy Toole*, and serves as a mentor for the WGA Vets Writing Project and Write Girl. Her poetry has appeared in *The Portland Review, Rosebud, Ellipsis...art and literature, Soundings East, Studio One, The Chaffin Journal, Eclipse*, and *Folly* among others. Deborah resides in Los Angeles with her husband, David Streit.

Phyllis Grilikhes is a writer, former dancer, classical musician, and psychologist on the faculty at City College of San Francisco. Her book, *To Set A Light In Every Tunnel: The Story of A Life*, is a poetic narrative. She has been published by *Willard & Maple, Cadillac Cicatrix, Eclipse, Manzanita Quarterly, Coe Review*, and *Cairn*. She finds that all that she does nourishes her writing life; nothing is wasted.

Award-winning video and performance poet, organizer, producer, and participant in the original development of the internationally-acclaimed, "Poetry Slam", **Jean Howard** has poetry published in over one hundred publications, including *Harper's Magazine, The Chicago Tribune*, and her own book, *Dancing In Your Mother's Skin* (Tia Chucha Press). Find out more about her at www.jeanhoward. com.

Judy Ireland's poetry benefits from the verdancy and barefaced authenticity of Midwest working class culture, as well as from the lush excesses of South Florida, where she currently lives and works. Her poems have been, or are soon to be, published in *Folio, Saranac Review, Hotel Amerika, Coe Review, Cold Mountain Review, Chaffin Journal*, and *Grasslimb*. Her chapbook, *Cement Shoes*, was listed as a finalist for the 2010 Split Oak Press Chapbook Contest and the 2010 Palettes and Quills Poetry Chapbook Contest.

Alexis Ivy is from Boston, Massachusetts. Her most recent poems have appeared in *Main Street Rag, Off The Coast, Spare Change News, Common Ground Review*, and are upcoming in *The Santa Fe Literary Review, The Chiron Review, Tar River*, and *Eclipse*. She is currently seeking to publish her first manuscript, *Romance with Small-Time Crooks*.

Jeffrey N. Johnson's short stories have appeared or are forthcoming in *The Sewanee Review, The Connecticut Review, The Evansville Review, South Dakota Review, Night Train Magazine, North Atlantic Review, The Summerset Review, The Distillery, Licking River Review, Potomac Review*, and *Aethlon: The Journal of Sport Literature*. His poems have appeared in *South Carolina Review* and *Gargoyle Magazine*. He's a fellow of the Virginia Center for the Creative Arts (VCCA), and a recipient of a Creative Fellow grant from the Mid-Atlantic Arts Foundation. He lives in Alexandria, Virginia, with his wife and twin babies.

William Jolliff serves as a professor of English at George Fox University. His chapbook, *Whatever Was Ripe*, won the 1997 Bright Hill Press poetry competition. His edited collection, *The Poetry of John Greenleaf Whittier: A Readers' Edition*, was published by Friends United Press. Bill has published critical articles and poems in over a hundred periodicals, including *Northwest Review, Southern Humanities Review, Midwest Quarterly, Christianity and Literature*, and *Appalachian Journal*. His most recent chapbook is *Searching for a White Crow* (2009).

Robert King recently won the Grayson Books Chapbook Competition with his manuscript, *Rodin & Co.* His first book, *Old Man Laughing* (Ghost Road Press), was a finalist for the 2008 Colorado Book Award in Poetry. He lives in Greeley, Colorado, where he directs the website www.ColoradoPoetsCenter.org.

Margery Kreitman is a playwright, solo performance artist, and author of creative non-fiction. Her full-length comedies, one acts, and sketch comedy revues have been produced in San Francisco, Los Angeles and New York. Her short stories have appeared in *Gargoyle, Pisgah Review, Rockhurst Review,* and *Dos Passos Review.* Margery is the creator/producer of *LGBT Writes!*—short, funny, personal essays produced at The Marsh Café in San Francisco. She has taught Theater Arts for children and young adults at ACT, The Academy of Art College, and Bay Area public schools, and privately for adults.

John P. Kristofco is from Wooster, Ohio, and is a professor of English and dean of Wayne College in nearby Orrville. His poetry and short stories have appeared in over a hundred different publications, including *Folio, Sojourn, Cimarron Review, Rattle, The Red Rock Review, Blueline,* and *Poem.* He has published one collection of poetry, *A Box of Stones* with another, *Apparitions,* due out soon.

Vivian Lawry is Appalachian by birth, a social psychologist by training, and a writer by passion. She writes magical realism, memoir, literary fiction, and murder mysteries. Her work has appeared or is forthcoming in *Aljembic, Apalachee Review, Art Times, The Binnacle, Chelsea, The Chrysalis Reader, The Connecticut Review, descant, The Dos Passos Review, The Distillery, Drumvoices, Happy, The Hurricane*

Review, Licking River Review, Lullwater Review, North Atlantic Review, North Dakota Quarterly, Oregon East, Phoebe, RE:AL, Reflections Literary Journal, RiverSedge, Seems, Studio One, Talking River Review, Westview, Willard & Maple, and *Xavier Review*. Visit her website at www.vivianlawry.com.

Yvonne Higgins Leach received her Bachelor of Arts in English from Washington State University in 1983 and a Master of Fine Arts from Eastern Washington University in 1986. Her work has appeared in *South Dakota Review, South Carolina Review, Spoon River Poetry Review, Cimarron Review, Phantasmagoria, West Wind Review, Willow Review, Arnazella, Owen Wister Review, Phoebe and Pearl*, among others. She works in Communications at Boeing Commercial Airplanes and lives in Snohomish, WA on five acres with her daughter.

Eleanore Lee has written poetry and fiction for many years in addition to working her day job as a legislative analyst for the University of California system. Her work has appeared in a range of journals, including *Atlanta Review, The Portland Review*, and *The Rambler*. She has also worked as an editor at Columbia Teachers College and as a stringer for *Time* magazine.

Karin Lin-Greenberg has stories published in or forthcoming from journals including *The Antioch Review, Epoch*, and *The North American Review*. She is currently working on a novel.

Evan Lottich grew up in Iowa, went to Europe and the Philippines in WWII, got a BA under the GI Bill, taught in high schools, and is presently retired from the Oregon Dept. of Human Resources.

Angie Macri's recent work appears or is forthcoming in *Cave Wall*, *RHINO*, and *Third Coast*, among other journals, and is included in Best New Poets 2010. A recipient of an individual artist fellowship from the Arkansas Arts Council, she teaches in Little Rock.

Teresa Milbrodt received her MFA in Creative Writing from Bowling Green State University. Her short story collection, *Bearded Women: Stories*, will be published by Chizine Publications in Fall 2011. Milbrodt's stories have appeared in *Nimrod*, *North American Review*, *Crazyhorse*, *The Cream City Review*, *Hayden's Ferry Review*, and *New Orleans Review*, among other literary journals. Several of her stories have also been nominated for a Pushcart Prize. She is an Assistant Professor of Creative Writing at Western State College of Colorado.

Iris Miller began writing poetry when she retired from teaching art in the City School District of Rochester, New York. She has a practice in shamanic healing and guided personal imagery, and occasionally works in paint or collage. Her poems have appeared in *The Sow's Ear Poetry Review*, *Nimrod*, *The South Carolina Review*, *Sou'wester*, *The Comstock Review*, and various anthologies.

Dr. William Miller lives and writes in the French Quarter of New Orleans. His fifth collection of poetry was published by The Mellen Poetry Press (2011). Individual poems have appeared in *The Southern Review*, *Shenandoah*, *Tar River Poetry*, and *Prairie Schooner*. He has also published twelve books for children, including *The Bus Ride* (with an introduction by Rosa Parks).

Ellen Birkett Morris is a poet and fiction writer based in Louisville, Kentucky. Her poetry has appeared in journals including *Gastronomica*, *Inscape*, *Alimentum*, *Juked*, and *The Pedestal Magazine*. Her poem Origins was nominated for the 2006 Pushcart Prize.

Lorna Nakell is a graphic designer and illustrator specializing in the publishing industry. She has a fondness for children's books, fine art publications, and singing karaoke. Currently she resides in Portland, Oregon, with her husband, son, and two cats—Kiwi and Mango.

Bethany Reid's poems have recently appeared in *Alembic*, *Superstition Review*, *Blackbird*, *The Sun*, *Calyx*, *Stringtown*, and *Pontoon*. She teaches American literature and creative writing at Everett Community College, north of Seattle, Washington, and blogs at www.awritersalchemy.blogspot.com.

An Oklahoman by birth, a Californian by choice, **Marilyn Ringer** retreats to an island in Maine for a month once a year to hike and write. Her poems have appeared or are forthcoming in: *Nimrod*, *Red Wheelbarrow*, *Eclectica*, *Meridian Anthology of Contemporary Poetry*, *Quiddity*, *Eclipse*, *RiverSedge*, *River Oak Review*, *Poet Lore*, *Porcupine*, *Left Curve*, *Milk Money*, and numerous other journals.

Poems by **J. Stephen Rhodes** have appeared in *Shenandoah*, *Tar River Poetry*, and *The International Poetry Review*, among others. His poetry collection, *The Time I Didn't Know What to Do Next*, was recently published by Wind Publications. He holds an MFA from the University of Southern Maine-Stonecoast, and a Ph.D. in theology from Emory University.

Hannah Selinger holds a BA in English and Comparative Literature from Columbia University, as well as an MFA in Creative Writing from Emerson College, where she was a Presidential Merit Fellow. Her work has appeared in *RiverSedge, Eclipse, Zone 3, Pennsylvania English, The South Carolina Review, The South Dakota Review,* and *Lullwater Review.*

Gina Troisi is a graduate of the the University of Maine's Stonecoast MFA Program. Her creative nonfiction has appeared in *Best New Writing 2010, PMSpoemmemoirstory Literary Journal, Room Magazine, Hope Whispers, The Concho River Review,* and *Compass Rose.* She currently lives in Dover, New Hampshire, where she tends bar in order to support her writing.

Karol M. Wasylyshyn, President of Leadership Development Forum, is a clinical and consulting psychologist specializing in leadership development. In addition to her professional writing, she is currently working on a leadership book based on the core behaviors she has observed in business executives over the last 30 years. Original case examples of these behaviors are presented through her poetry.

Christy Wise is the author of *A Mouthful of Rivets: Women at Work in World War II.* Her essays have received several awards and are published in numerous publications, including *Inscape, Bayou Magazine, Oasis Journal 2008,* and *Spot Literary Magazine.* Her essay "Memory Book," published in *Bayou 51,* was selected as a Notable Essay by Best American Essays. A native Californian, she lives in Washington, DC where she is working on a collection of essays and completing a master of liberal studies at Georgetown University.

Visit

CLACKAMAS LITERARY REVIEW

clackamasliteraryreview.org
facebook.com/clackamasliteraryreview

Contact
clr@clackamas.edu

CLACKAMAS LITERARY REVIEW

the finest writing for the best readers

Clackamas Literary Review has been committed to bringing you the best writing from around the world since 1997. Subscribe now to receive the latest and forthcoming issues.

Clackamas Literary Review

	1 year	$10
_____	2 years	$18
_____	3 years	$26

Name _____

Address _____

City / State / Zip _____

Email _____

Send this form and check or money order to:

Clackamas Literary Review
English Department
Clackamas Community College
19600 Molalla Avenue
Oregon City, Oregon 97045